BURIED ALIVE

A few bullets banged into the rocks along the tunnel, but Slocum just rolled over, got to his feet and made his way deeper into the maze. He had made enough turns in the mine to protect his back. As he walked, he kept shining his light up at the ceiling. That was where the exit would be.

Flashes of blue sky alerted Slocum that he had found his way out. He moved into the stope, studied it for a few seconds, then worked his way up. It took close to ten minutes before he heaved himself the final few feet and out onto the side of the hill. Below him stood several of Wall's men.

Slocum measured the distance and started thinking about picking them off one by one.

Then he saw another man struggling up the hill. He carried a large wooden box.

Dynamite. Wall had decided to bury Slocum alive.

"That works both ways," Slocum said softly. He settled down and began firing.

OTHER BOOKS BY JAKE LOGAN

JAKE LOGAN

SLOCUM AND THE RAILROAD BARON

BERKLEY BOOKS, NEW YORK

SLOCUM AND THE RAILROAD BARON

A Berkley Book / published by arrangement with
the author

PRINTING HISTORY
Berkley edition / February 1992

ISBN: 0-425-13187-4

A BERKLEY BOOK® TM 757,375
Berkley Books are published by The Berkley Publishing Group,
200 Madison Avenue, New York, New York 10016.
The name "BERKLEY" and the "B" logo
are trademarks belonging to Berkley Publishing Corporation.

SLOCUM AND THE RAILROAD BARON

1

The trail dust was so thick in his mouth that John Slocum couldn't even spit it out. He took off his battered gray Stetson and brushed some of the dirt from the front of his duster. He vanished in a swirling, choking cloud of brown. Coughing, he slipped from the saddle and hit the ground, glad to feel solid earth under his feet again. The roan he had bought in Denver was a steady horse, one of the best he had come across in a long while, but living astride the animal for two solid days was hell. He was glad to be out of the saddle and near enough to a saloon that he almost let out a whoop of joy.

Slocum stared at the roan, sighed, and then led the horse down Central City's main street to a small but well-kept livery. He signaled to a tow-headed boy lounging on a hay bale just inside the barn, whittling away at a slip of pine.

"Give the horse a good rubdown and then some grain," Slocum said. He reached into his vest pocket and pulled out a small coin. He flipped the silver coin to the boy, who deftly grabbed it.

"That'll be a dollar, mister, not any twelve and a half cents."

"I know. That's for you," Slocum said, sizing up the urchin. For all the hair in wild disarray and the tattered clothing, the boy had the look about him of someone responsible beyond his years. "I'll match the bit if you do a good job. And here's the board." Slocum fumbled out a silver cartwheel and sent it after the bit piece. The boy snared it with equal dexterity.

"You got it, mister. This horse is gonna get the best damn rubdown you ever saw. And currying!"

Slocum nodded, smiled slightly, and felt his lips crack. The dryness of the Colorado early autumn was enough to turn his skin to leather and his guts to powder. He turned and retraced his steps to the saloon. The time spent going to the livery hadn't been wasted, as much as he needed a drink. It never paid to let an animal go untended. That roan was a good horse and might save his life—again.

Slocum had been been jumped twice on his way to Central City from Denver. Once he was sure it was a sheriff's posse intent on finding any lawbreaker, no matter who. He had doubled back on them, confused his trail, and done a half dozen different things to throw the posse off the track. It must have worked, because a band of five outlaws had tried to waylay him less than a day later. Slocum didn't have to guess that the posse was after these men, but it did him little good to stand and talk the matter over with them. Shots had been exchanged, and he had ridden like the very wind, the roan giving him more than he would have expected.

He owed that horse a night's rest and all the oats it could eat. But now it was time to tend to his own needs. His belly rubbed up against his spine and his mouth was worse than the inside of a bale of cotton. First a little whiskey, then some dinner.

Slocum pushed through the saloon doors and stood, studying the crowd inside before going in. He took a step in and then stopped to stare at the floor. A woman's face had been painted there. She stared up with a sly expression, a knowing look, almost winking to let him know that this was the place he sought.

"Come on over, fella. Have a drink on the house." The barkeep pulled out a bottle and poured Slocum a shot.

"What's the occasion?" Slocum asked. "Not often I find anyone willing to buy me a drink these days."

The barkeep stepped back a half pace and squinted at Slocum. "You ain't with the railroad?"

"Can't say that I am," Slocum allowed. "Does that mean I don't get the free drink?"

"Nothing of the kind," the barkeep said. He squinted a little harder, showing how much he needed glasses for work this close up. "You just looked like one of them cayuses Parsons hires on."

"Parsons?" Slocum asked. He sipped at the whiskey, expecting it to have the kick of a mule. It slid down his gullet softer than a summer breeze. He knocked back the rest of the drink and let it warm his innards.

"Anthony Parsons, the owner of the Rocky Mountain Rail Line. Surprised you ain't heard of him. Most everyone in these parts has." The barkeep squinted at Slocum again, as if considering how much of a lie Slocum was handing him.

"Just passing through," Slocum said. "Don't know anything about railroads or this Parsons." He signaled that he wanted another drink from the same bottle, then turned and looked at the crowded saloon. If he hadn't been so intent on the woman's face painted on the floor, he would have seen the railroad workers right away. Sunburned, burly, and rawboned, these men worked hard and drank even harder. And the faint Irish brogue Slocum made out from their talk clinched the identification.

One of the men crashed into him. Slocum stepped back, waiting to see if this was going to be the start of a fight. He was tired and didn't cotton much to fighting with these men. For them it was relaxation. For him it would mean someone would have to die. He was tired, banged up from too many close calls, and didn't have the strength left to get into a knock-down drag-out fight. Killing would only complicate his life, and right now he wanted to keep things as simple as he could.

"Sorry, mister." The man peered at Slocum through alcohol-fogged eyes. "Ye workin' for Mr. Bergstrom, now, are ye?"

Slocum just shook his head. The man didn't seem to notice. He clapped Slocum on the back so hard it jerked him forward.

"Buy this man a drink. He's workin' for me boss, he is!"

"No, I—" Slocum clamped his mouth shut. Others were drifting closer. Slocum didn't want to start anything. He'd finish his drink, and the one the railroad man had just bought him, and then leave the saloon. As much as he needed the whiskey to wet his whistle, he needed food and sleep more.

"Drink up. We're in town on a toot!"

This produced a long round of laughter. Slocum smiled wryly and lifted the shot glass. "To Mr. Bergstrom," he said. "Long may he be able to pay for your drinks."

This brought out another round of applause and laughter. The men began pushing closer to the bar, demanding more whiskey. Slocum finished his drink and let it pool warmly in his gut. It was time to move on. He started to leave, but a huge arm circled his shoulders and held him in place.

"Not thinkin' of goin' off so soon, are ye, now?"

The man's breath was enough to gag a maggot. His eyes were bloodshot and he wobbled mightily, even supporting himself against the well-polished bar.

"Not before I buy you a drink," Slocum said. He dropped a silver dollar on the bar. "Give 'em all a drink," Slocum said. This brought a cheer of approval, and Slocum wondered what wouldn't. These men were bound and determined to have a good time.

He let one push him away from the bar to get his drink. Slocum used this as a way to start for the door. He got halfway there when he found his way blocked by another mountain of a man, this one with a long brown handlebar mustache waxed so tight it looked as if it wanted to scream. The tips wiggled as the man's upper lip quivered. But it was the set to the mouth that warned Slocum that trouble was on the way.

"You," the man said, stabbing his finger into Slocum's chest. "You been drinkin' with that scum? You one of Bergstrom's men?"

"Just passing through," Slocum said.

"Hear that, boys?" The man with the mustache turned to his three companions. "He says he's just passing through. Does he look like he's lying? I think he is."

Slocum stepped back a pace and sized up the four men. It didn't look good. All four wore their six-shooters with authority. The worn grips and the slick leather holsters told of long use—deadly use. They were gunmen looking for someone to kill.

"Who might you be?" Slocum asked, not really caring. He tried to figure the best way of getting out of the saloon alive. Drawing down on the men wasn't the way to do it. He might get the leader with the waxed mustache, but the other three would have cleared leather and let lead fly before he could turn his attention to them. Four against one was sucker odds.

"Emmett Wall, that's who I be," the man said. His mustache twitched even more. "I'm foreman for the Rocky Mountain Rail Line."

"He works for Mr. Parsons," the man on the left put in. Slocum didn't turn to face the man. He knew this trick. The instant his attention wavered from Emmett Wall, the foreman would go for his pistol. Slocum's cold green eyes locked on Wall's muddy brown ones and refused to leave. It was a war of wills, neither man intending to break.

"Who are you?"

"Nobody you'd care to know," Slocum said. "I'm getting ready to leave town."

"Just passing through," taunted another of the gunmen.

By now the cacophony in the saloon was dying down. The railroad workers saw what was going on.

"Been drinkin' with this scum," Wall said loudly. "I take that to mean you're scum, just like them. Ain't nobody what works for the Denver and Utah Railroad that's not lower than a snake's belly. Why don't you crawl out of here?"

Slocum forced himself to relax. He was going to have to shoot his way out.

"You're full of shit, Wall!" called a man behind Slocum. "You man enough to stand up to him in a fair fight?"

Slocum saw the slow grin spread on Wall's face. His mustache twitched even more. The notion of a fistfight was more to his liking than shooting it out. Slocum wasn't sure if he wanted the fight to go that way. He was dog-tired from riding nonstop from Denver and he had a cracked rib that hadn't healed completely. It had been hell the time he'd spent in Colorado, and he wanted nothing more than to keep riding west until he got to Utah. Mormon country was more peaceable and would give him a chance to recuperate.

"Yeah, Wall, you fight him, unless you're too chicken-shit." Others took up the cry.

"Let's do it," Wall said, shucking off his gun belt. Slocum considered his chances now. It would be his draw and quick fire against Wall's three companions. The odds still didn't favor him getting out of the saloon alive. Fighting Wall looked to be his only chance. Slocum unbuckled his soft leather cross-draw holster and held it out. Someone behind him took it.

And Slocum was already ducking the meaty fist driving square for his nose. He let Wall's blow pass his face, then stepped in, his fists driving hard and fast for the man's midriff. Slocum thought he was pounding against granite. Every blow landed and every one bounced back from Wall's heavily muscled belly.

Slocum danced away and sidestepped another powerful but poorly delivered blow. He tried to keep the railroad workers from distracting him. They were cheering him on, making bets, goading Wall into making a mistake. Slocum had the added burden of keeping watch on the three gunmen with Emmett Wall. If the fight looked to be going against their boss, they were likely to end it with a few well-placed bullets.

"Come on and fight, you lily-livered son of a bitch," puffed Wall. He waded in, swinging wildly. Any one of the blows would have felled an elephant. Slocum avoided them, some by the barest margin. Once Wall's left fist sailed by his cheek, a large gold ring opening up a shallow cut. The blood spurted everywhere and made the crowd go wild.

But the minor wound afforded Slocum the chance he needed. Wall thought the damage was worse than it was and stopped for a moment to gloat. Slocum gauged his distance, stepped up, and swung with all his might. His fist struck Wall on the temple. The man went down like a tree with its base sawed out from under it.

Slocum didn't repeat Wall's mistake of gloating. He doubled over, hit the floor and rolled, coming up next to the man holding his ebony-handled Colt Navy. Slocum shoved the man back, drawing his six-shooter as he did so. He had the pistol cocked and aimed before any of the three gunmen could respond.

"Get him out of here," cried the barkeep, pointing at Wall's feebly twitching body. "I told you guys from the Rocky Mountain Rail Line not to come in here lookin' for trouble."

"They surely did find it tonight!" chortled a hairy, compactly built man beside Slocum. "Go on, put away your piece. You're among friends. Parsons ain't got a claim on your life. These are all Clarence Bergstrom men!"

Slocum panted hard to get his breath back. This was a problem riding through Colorado. The damned cities were so high up in the mountains they robbed you of wind in nothing flat.

"Heard ye say ye was just passin' through. Let me buy ye a drink. Let's talk this over, eh?"

Slocum let the man guide him toward a table near a window. Slocum sat so that he could look out the window into the street and still keep a watch on what happened inside the saloon. Only when he had his gun belt back on and the Colt loose in his holster did he accept the drink the man offered.

"Much obliged," Slocum said. He winced as the whiskey stung his mouth. Somewhere during the fight he had bitten the inside of his cheek.

"I'm Gus Maguire, Mr. Bergstrom's foreman out on the line."

Slocum said nothing. He wasn't pleased to meet Emmett Wall's opposite number. That kept him squarely between the two warring camps. All he wanted to do was move on, leaving Central City and this night's unpleasantness behind.

"You saw the kind of men Wall surrounds himself with. Killers, the lot of 'em. Mr. Bergstrom's not taken that route. He wants to win fair and square without intimidatin'."

"Good for him."

Maguire coughed to clear his throat. He looked at Slocum, the seriousness in his eyes telling what he wanted long before the words came. "Mr. Bergstrom's not the sort of man to hire killers, but he needs help out at the site."

"I'm not a hired gun," Slocum said.

"You're mighty handy with that," Maguire said, indicating the Colt. "I can tell by the way ye move—and ye fight good enough to hold your own with any man jack in this place."

"I'm not looking for a job." Slocum leaned back and stared into the darkened street. Gaslights cast flickering shadows and turned Central City into an eerie place. He blinked twice when a vision of loveliness crossed his field of vision. The woman stopped at the window and peered in, her perfectly formed lips turning up in a hint of a smile intended just for him. She made a tentative gesture toward him, then turned and hurried off.

Gus Maguire looked back over his shoulder and saw her.

"She's quite an eyeful, ain't she? That there's Melody Bergstrom, Mr. Bergstrom's daughter. She spends a fair amount of time out at the site."

"Do tell." Slocum had seldom seen a woman so lovely, but her presence at the railroad construction site meant little to him.

"I'll make you a wager," said Maguire. "One hand."

"What?" Slocum fought to get his concentration back to the matter at hand. He had been thinking how long it had been since he'd had any woman, much less one as attractive as Melody Bergstrom.

"I can tell you're a sporting man, one who enjoys a wager now and again."

"So?"

"So, here is my proposition. Mr. Bergstrom's not lookin' for killers, but he does sorely need a man who can guard what's rightly ours. We're all expert at drillin' in hard rock and layin' track, but we ain't no match for Emmett Wall's kind."

"What's the wager?" Slocum asked, in spite of his better judgment.

"One hundred dollars. Gold." Maguire pulled out a bag of dust and dropped it on the table with a dull thud that rang like a bell in Slocum's ears. He had a bit of money, but a hundred dollars in gold dust would go a long way toward getting him out of Colorado. "One hand, seven card stud poker."

"I win, I get the gold. What if I lose?"

"You come to work for the Denver and Utah until we're through Widowmaker Pass."

"How long will that be?" Slocum asked.

"Depends on if we're allowed to do our work or if we have to fight off Wall and his henchmen all the time. What say ye?"

Slocum looked up and saw the woman peering inside once more. She had long, dark brown hair that flowed like a pure, clean river over her shoulders. Her lips were pursed just so, and her eyes twinkled. Slocum heaved a sigh and said, "You shuffle; I'll cut."

Gus Maguire let out a whoop and motioned to the barkeep for a deck of cards. Slocum's attention was divided between the way Maguire opened the new deck and shuffled and Melody Bergstrom watching from outside.

"There," Maguire said, sliding the deck to Slocum. Slocum cut the deck three times, just to be sure, then watched the railroad foreman deal out two cards down, four up, and then a final down.

"Looks like I got you," Maguire said. "I got three deuces showing. Might have a fourth in the hole. What's it going to be?"

Slocum checked his cards. He had a flush, three of the cards in the hole.

"Let's see."

Gus Maguire turned over his hole cards and showed nothing more. He had the three deuces. "So?" he asked. "Let's see yours."

Slocum looked at the flush again, then remembered the inviting look Melody Bergstrom had given him. Slocum damned himself for being such a fool. This wasn't any business of his, and what did he know about building railroads? Still, the pressure on getting to Utah wasn't *that* great. It wasn't as if he had a posse on his tail.

He pulled the rest of the cards in from the table and shoved them into the deck.

"You got yourself a guard—just till you get through Widowmaker Pass."

2

"Yes, sir, it surely is good having ye with us, Slocum," Gus Maguire said. Slocum hoped the man wouldn't slap him on the back again. Every huge thump sent tremors of pain through him. Slocum had been thrown from a horse just east of Denver almost two weeks earlier when it had stepped into a prairie dog hole. He'd shot the horse and limped into Denver, bedraggled, tired, and angry at losing such a fine animal. The time spent in Denver hadn't done much to soothe him, either.

He had been in a series of poker games where his luck had grown progressively worse. Slocum had decided to leave while he still had a few dollars in his pocket. He looked over his shoulder at the table by the window and knew he might have made a mistake letting Melody Bergstrom's loveliness sway him into helping out Maguire. The gold would have been his, fair and square. He could have done anything he wanted with it bouncing at his belt. Now he was obligated to help Bergstrom build his damned railroad, at least through Widowmaker Pass.

"What's the problem getting the track laid?" Slocum asked the foreman. Maguire cleared his throat and moved closer, as if this would keep the dozen other men around them from overhearing.

"It's like this. There's a big government reward for gettin' a road over the divide and into the town of Cameron. Mr. Bergstrom knows he has the best route, one he can run cheaper once he gets it built."

"And Parsons's route is going to cost more to run and maintain. I assume the government will be footing the bill for transporting everything once the tracks are down."

"That's it, God bless ye for bein' so sharp. Parsons is takin' the easy way through, but it's no good for the people in Cameron and beyond dependin' on supplies. Mr. Bergstrom intends to run the road himself, and he can keep it open year-round."

"So we get through this Widowmaker Pass and the award goes to Clarence Bergstrom?" Slocum thought this was too easy. There had to be more.

"Parsons is takin' his track through the Grand Gorge, a place needin' a mighty trestle. The man ain't got the sense God gave a goose. All you need to do is look at the green, knotted wood he's usin' and you'd know it'll collapse inside a year."

"So he's going through Grand Gorge and you're having to blast through a mountain pass?" Slocum had the basics of the situation down, and he didn't like the sound of it. Accidents happened when hard-rock blasting was needed, and Slocum didn't even like to think of the backbreaking labor it took laying steel rail. He wasn't the kind of man to admit there were many better than he at any chore, but this was work he would avoid whenever possible.

"That's the way it is," Gus Maguire said. Slocum waited. The rest would come out eventually. All he had to do was let the foreman get around to it in his own way. The truth wasn't long in coming. Maguire finished his drink and said, "They been stealin' us blind. They come ridin' in when we least expect it and take our food, our spikes, anything they can. Don't rightly think they go far with the heavier items, so we're hangin' onto our drillin' equipment."

"They just dump the spikes and other supplies to keep you from using them?"

"That's the way I see it, and Mr. Bergstrom agrees. We tried puttin' out a sentry or two. Never seen the poor sonsabitches again. Parsons's men done 'em in, mark my word." Maguire coughed again, considered another drink, and decided against it. "This ain't gonna sway you none, is it, Slocum?"

"I made a deal," Slocum said. "I don't know what kind of man you think I am, but I don't go back on my word."

"I knew ye were our kind of man," Maguire said. They stood and started out of the noisy saloon. "This has a fortune ridin' on it. You stick with Mr. Bergstrom, and a part of it can be yours."

"Subsidized rail freight?" Slocum snorted in disgust. He wasn't the kind to stick around after the track was laid.

"More'n that, laddie buck. The government is payin' a quarter of a million dollars to the line what gets over the divide first *and* it gets alternate sections of land. Pick one or two of those and you'd be a wealthy man. Mark my words."

Slocum saw that the stakes in this race were high. He also guessed that Bergstrom had little chance of winning against an unscrupulous operator like Anthony Parsons. Bergstrom played fair and wanted to build a business. All Parsons wanted was a quick profit.

Slocum had to pause for a moment and figure out what it was he wanted. The pay was an inducement, but he could have had one hundred dollars in gold without going through this charade. He didn't even know Bergstrom's daughter. Maybe she didn't care for drifters like him. Slocum snorted in the cold mountain air and sent silvery plumes of condensed breath knifing out from his nostrils. Maybe no decent woman would. His life had been anything but pure.

Riding with Quantrill's Raiders wasn't something Slocum was proud of. They had been a bloody-handed bunch, and he hadn't been the gentlest of them. But the Lawrence, Kansas, raid had turned his stomach. Killing women and children had nothing to do with fighting a war, and his complaints had left him with a bullet in the belly. By the time he had recovered enough to travel, the war was nearly over. And his troubles were just beginning.

His parents were dead for the better part of a year and his brother Robert had died during Pickett's Charge. The life of a gentleman farmer in Calhoun, Georgia, appealed to him after the death and blood he had seen, but a carpetbagger judge had other notions. No taxes had been paid on the farm, he claimed. The Reconstruction judge and his hired gunman had ridden in; Slocum had ridden out that afternoon, leaving twin graves on a hill above the springhouse. Since then he had been running from a passel of warrants. Judge killing, even when the judge was crooked as a dog's hind leg, was a crime no one forgot or forgave.

Too many wanted posters, some deserved and some not, floated around the West. What woman could stand the notion that the next knock on the door might be a marshal come to take her man to the gallows?

"You're mighty thoughtful, Slocum. Anything the matter?"

"Not more than usual," Slocum said. "How long you reckon it's going to take to lay track across Widowmaker Pass?"

Maguire didn't answer directly. "We been workin' our tails off to get the way cleared and a solid roadbed blasted."

"And?" prodded Slocum. "You talking about a week or a month? I'm not staying if I have to spend the winter in the Rockies. I've done that before and damned near lost my toes to frostbite."

"We'll be over the pass before the first snow. As dry as it's been this year, snow might come late. But there's something more to your job that I wasn't tellin' ye."

"What is it?" Slocum readied himself for the worst, wondering if it would be an adequate excuse for him to simply get on his horse and ride off.

"There've been threats. Nothin' we can prove to any sheriff, but we know the one responsible."

"Parsons," Slocum said. "I'm supposed to be bodyguard to Mr. Bergstrom?"

"Clarence Bergstrom would never stand for it, sir!" Maguire straightened until the top of his head came up almost to Slocum's shoulder. The hairy foreman bristled all over like a stepped-on porcupine. "He prides himself on bein' able to take any risk his men take. That's what makes everyone so loyal to him."

"If not Bergstrom, then—" Slocum's words cut off and a slow smile crossed his lips. He was beginning to like the job more and more, and he hadn't even seen the construction site yet.

"Miss Bergstrom. She insists on staying out here rather than back in Denver where she belongs. She's got an ornery streak in her, and stubborn! She can out-stubborn any mule what ever lived. She says the family fortunes are all tied up in getting the track laid, so she's not gonna waste her time back in Denver. She helps out at the camp, sometimes with the meals, mostly with patchin' up the men when they get injured on the job."

Slocum laughed. Bergstrom must have considerable malingering if Melody Bergstrom was doctoring the men.

"This isn't a problem with ye, then, Slocum?" Maguire looked at Slocum as if to detect some sign of regret for giving his word as he had done. He saw none.

"Are we heading out to the camp now?" Slocum asked. "I've been riding hard for two days and I'm bushed. I could stay in Central City and then ride out the first thing in the morning."

"Do that," Maguire said. "I've got to go to the sheriff's office and talk with him. Before sunup half my crew'll be in the lockup." As if emphasizing his words, two men crashed through the saloon's double doors and fell heavily in the street, beating at each other with blows that would have dropped a buffalo, had they landed. Maguire said nothing and went to the wrestling pair. He measured his distance and then kicked as hard as he could. One man let out a howl of injured dignity and swung around, rolling in the dirt to face his new attacker.

"Come on, ye mangy cayuse. Come on and take a swing," Maguire shouted. "I told ye no fightin' whilst in town. If'n ye think ye can take me, ye can have my job and welcome to it."

Slocum watched as the sober Maguire deliberately punched and jabbed, reducing the man to a pile of quivering flesh in less than a minute. The others in his crew howled and hooted, urging them on. Slocum wasn't sure who the men were backing, and it might not have mattered. They just wanted to see a fight.

Slocum turned and went toward the livery to see if the stableboy had taken care of the roan. He hadn't gotten halfway down the street when he heard Gus Maguire's bull-throated roar. He turned and saw the foreman waving frantically. Slocum frowned, not knowing what was happening.

"They took her, Slocum. Those owlhoots got her!"

"What are you talking about?"

Maguire was out of breath. A half dozen of his men had gathered around. One of them, hardly a boy but with shoulders broader than an axe handle blurted out, "I seen it! I seen them takin' Miss Bergstrom. They caught her on her way from the general store. She'd just bought supplies and they tried breakin' open the bags of flour and throwin' it in the street."

"When was this?" asked Slocum. The boy wasn't about to stop in the middle of his story to answer questions.

"She tried to stop them. She got real mad and grabbed up a buggy whip and laid into that Emmett Wall. Got him square across the face, she did."

"What happened?" Slocum demanded. The coldness of his voice and the set to his body made the boy pale. He swallowed hard and tried to speak, then stopped and let Maguire finish for him.

"Those bastards took her, Slocum. Wall and his three henchmen kidnapped her! What ye gonna do about it?"

Slocum looked around the circle of men and knew that rescuing Melody Bergstrom was going to be up to him.

3

Slocum's mind raced, considering all the possibilities. "Are you sure they took her? Could she have gone off on her own, maybe back to your camp?"

"Mister, I *seen* it," the young man insisted. The way he shook with emotion told Slocum he had seen something frightening enough to rattle him. Slocum wasn't sure what kind of men Clarence Bergstrom had working for him, but from what he'd seen, they weren't liars. He thought Gus Maguire might be prone to exaggerate a bit for the sake of a good story, but he wouldn't outright lie.

"Did you see which way they went?"

"The four of them took Miss Melody and rode out that way." The man pointed into the darkness, giving Slocum no hint as to the real direction the kidnappers had taken.

"I reckon they might be headin' for the Rocky Mountain Rail camp," Maguire said. "That don't make a good deal of sense to me, but ye can never say with those owlhoots. Sometimes I don't think that Emmett Wall has any common sense."

"If they took her to their construction camp," Slocum said, thinking hard, "how many men would there be there?"

"Maybe a hundred," Maguire answered. "What are ye sayin, Slocum?"

"Is Parsons the ransoming kind?" Slocum asked.

Maguire had to think on this for a moment, rubbing his stubbled chin. He finally shook his head. "I wouldn't put anything past him, but this is dangerous territory for him. He'd be itchin' to have the law called in. So far, everything he's done has been sneaky and underhanded, things we could never prove in a hundred years."

"It might just be that Wall has taken to runnin' the camp on his own. He's a wild one, he is," opined someone else. This caused the men to break into smaller groups to discuss the chance that Wall was actually the power in the Rocky Mountain camp. Slocum took Maguire aside.

"These men aren't up to going after them," he said.

Maguire heaved a deep sigh. "That's what I been tryin' to tell ye, Slocum. They're good railroad men. Not a one of them couldn't lay a mile of track a day all by his lonesome, but when it comes to something as fearsome as this—" Maguire shook his head sadly. Slocum didn't have to know who was responsible for getting the boss's daughter back.

He'd taken the job, knowing it wasn't going to be any Sunday social picnic. He just hadn't thought he'd have to start earning his keep this fast. The notion of riding on over the continental divide and getting to Utah appealed to him more than ever. This wasn't his fight.

"What ye plannin' on doing to get her back, Slocum?"

"Can't say. Got to find her first. Then I'll worry about rescuing her. Wall and the others might not have taken her to the construction camp."

"You want some help in this?" Maguire asked tentatively. From his tone, Slocum knew the blocky foreman wasn't exactly offering, but would go along if Slocum thought he was needed. Slocum considered the man's possible help and decided Gus Maguire was a man to have at his side in a fistfight but out on the trail, tracking by bright Colorado moonlight, he wouldn't be worth a bucket of spit.

"I'll see what can be done. If I need you, where's your camp?"

Relief spread over Maguire's round face. The man scratched some more at his stubbly chin, then hunkered down and traced out a crude map in the dust. "This here's Central City. Ye can see our company flag from the outskirts. Just ride on toward it until ye find a good sized road. It's the only one ye can take. Mr. Bergstrom's got things set up real nice out there."

"I'm sure he has," Slocum said dryly. He went and fetched his horse. He wished he could have given the animal a good night's rest, but that wasn't going to happen. For all that, Slocum wished he could have spent the night snoring so hard it chased the ticks out of his blanket. He saddled and mounted, riding out of Central City slowly.

He had expected a small group of the railroad workers to see him off. He didn't see even Maguire. As Slocum rode, he checked his Winchester and the Colt Navy slung at his side. The six-shooter carried only five rounds, the hammer resting on an empty cylinder. Before he reached the edge of the town, he had the sixth cylinder loaded. Slocum had the gut level feeling he was going to need all the firepower he could muster when he found the kidnappers.

Central City's lights were quickly behind him and the velvet night swallowed him whole. It took almost ten minutes before Slocum got his night vision and decided to take a good look at the ground. He wasn't sure tracking Wall and the others was going to be possible, even with the full moon hanging so high in the sky.

He dropped to his hands and knees and worked back and forth across the dusty road looking for some sign of recent passage. Slocum's nose found it before he saw the droppings alongside the road. The manure was still warm. A horse had passed by within the last half hour. Since he doubted anyone else was on the trail this late, that meant he was on the right track. He mounted and rode along slowly, ears straining for any hint of conversation between the men.

He hoped Melody Bergstrom might cry out and give them away, but he doubted Wall was so stupid that he'd let the woman ride along without a secure gag.

Every branching trail had to be checked. When the wind began kicking up, Slocum guessed the kidnappers were at least two hours ahead of him. Even in broad daylight, following them on the rocky road would have been a chore. Finding tiny scratches where a shod hoof had struck a rock was difficult enough. In the darkness it was almost impossible, and the dusty road held little in the way of tracks.

Slocum patted his roan and said softly, "We might be on a wild-goose chase, old boy. It might be better for us to hole up for the night and start looking again in the morning."

The horse snorted and stopped, eyeing something he saw on the trail. This was unlike the roan, who didn't spook at much of anything. Slocum calmed the horse, then dismounted. A broad smile crossed his lips. Luck was riding high on his shoulder this night. In the middle of the road, reflecting the moonlight, lay a silver conch and a length of leather cord. Slocum examined it and saw that the leather thong had been sawed through, as if someone had been tied with it and had spent a long time rubbing it back and forth across the silver conch. He put the ornament into his shirt pocket and kept walking. The dust in the road was churned up as if several horses had circled repeatedly. Slocum found another silver conch. He was on the right track.

He kept walking and found where the horses had left the road and headed across country. The going was rugged and the horses ahead had slipped repeatedly, but the riders had stayed in the saddle. Slocum led his horse uphill and was surprised to find a road at the top. The dirt path curled down the far side of the hill. He wondered why anyone would build a road to the top, then looked down into the far canyon and saw a sprawling construction camp. From this vantage point a sentry could watch every approach to the site.

He knew it didn't matter if Anthony Parsons was responsible for giving the orders to kidnap Melody Bergstrom or if Wall had simply acted on his own. Somewhere down there the woman was being held against her will. Slocum wasn't sure how he was going to find her, but he had come this far and wasn't going to turn back.

He sat on a rock, rolled a cigarette, and smoked while studying the lay of the land. Again luck was with him. Down at the base of the road leading to his overlook burned a small campfire. He counted the men around it and decided it was at least four and maybe five—and the fifth member simply sat while the others moved constantly. Since they were separated from the main camp, he could sneak up on them and take a quick look.

"Sorry to leave you here, old boy," Slocum said to his horse. He patted the animal's neck and tethered it near a patch of scrubby grass. It wasn't much, but would keep the horse from nickering and giving him away while he went down the hill.

Slocum checked his six-shooter again, toyed with the idea of carrying his rifle, and finally decided he could get by just fine with the side arm. He wasn't intending to get into a long, drawn out gunfight. If it came to that, he'd hightail it and go fetch Maguire and his crew.

He made his way down the steep road and found a large boulder that would shield him as he worked closer to the campsite. Before he had edged halfway around the large rock, voices came drifting back on the wind to him.

"It was a damnfool thing to do, Emmett," someone said. "You know Parsons ain't never gonna agree to it."

"Mr. Parsons is a businessman. He knows the value of having a pat hand." Slocum recognized the speaker as Emmett Wall. "Besides, we don't have to come right out and tell him we grabbed Bergstrom's daughter. All we want is to keep the Denver and Utah from making more than a few miles of track a day. If we can get the last of the timber for the bridge across the gorge before they reach

Widowmaker Pass, we've got 'em beat fourteen ways to Sunday."

"So all you want to do is slow them up?"

Slocum moved closer, flattening himself on the top of the rock. By the flickering light from the fire, he made out Wall and his three henchman. The fifth figure huddled on the far side, near a shallow arroyo. Slocum let the men talk while he slid back down the rock. He had seen enough to devise a plan. It would be dangerous, but leaving Melody Bergstrom in Wall's hands would be even more dangerous for the woman.

"We can fool around with her a little, can't we, Emmett?" asked one gunman. "Ain't nobody to tell, and who'd believe her?"

Slocum tried not to hurry and make a noise that would alert the four men. This was the kind of talk he'd been afraid of hearing. Melody Bergstrom might be better off dead than staying with them.

"Not yet. We'll palaver with her pa and see if that don't stop the Denver and Utah from moving too close to the pass. Is that all right with you li'l darlin'?"

Slocum peered up and saw Wall reach out to touch the woman's cheek. She savagely snapped at him. He pulled back and laughed. Then he slapped her hard enough to spin her around and drop her facedown on the ground. Slocum slid back to his belly and kept moving. Things might turn real ugly quick if he didn't get into a position where he could defend her.

"Let her be for now, boys," Wall said. "But you can all have her if her pa don't stop building his damned railroad." The way he laughed went beyond cruel. It was everything Slocum could do to keep from rising up and putting a bullet through the foreman's vile heart.

The other three subsided, contenting themselves with swapping lies about their sexual prowess and spitting into the fire. Slocum quieted his racing pulse, then spent the better part of fifteen minutes before he crawled into the shallow ravine running just a few feet from where Melody Bergstrom still lay on her stomach, face in hands, crying softly.

"Miss Bergstrom," Slocum whispered. "I've come to get you away from Wall and the others."

Her head snapped up and those lovely eyes he remembered from the saloon window fixed on him.

"Who are you?"

"Name's John Slocum. You saw me earlier tonight. I was with Gus Maguire. I just hired on."

"You're not a railroad man."

"Doesn't matter much what I am if I can get you away from them, now does it?"

"How do I know?" She shivered and looked up. In a low voice, she said, "It doesn't much matter if you're working for my father, does it? Anything is better than staying here."

Slocum grunted agreement as he worked up from the arroyo. He saw the way they had her roped to a stake. It looked like the way he'd put a lamb out to lure a puma. He reached behind him for the thick-bladed knife sheathed there. It took only a single quick cut to part the tough rope. Melody let out a sigh of relief as the ropes left her leg. A huge bruise had formed where the rope had cut into her flesh.

"What do you want me to do?"

"I can't shoot it out with them," Slocum said. "We're too near their main camp."

"They can't expect much help from that front," Melody said. Seeing Slocum's frown, she added, "Most of Parsons's workmen are Chinese. If too many of the guards leave, Parsons might have his entire construction crew run away."

Slocum didn't bother telling her it would take only three or four more armed men to make their escape impossible. He watched for several seconds, and saw that two of the men had tipped their hats over their eyes and laid back, already asleep. Wall and another man sat and talked quietly.

"Take off your clothes," Slocum said suddenly.

"I beg your pardon!"

"Do it if you want to get away from here. Just your dress." Slocum was already at work gathering what scrub he could to fill the woman's clothing. Melody Bergstrom was reluctant but obeyed, constantly looking from Slocum to Wall and back, as if sure this was just another ploy on the railroad foreman's part. She silently handed over her dress. Slocum slid into the ravine and worked for several minutes getting the vegetation crammed into the dress. It was far too lumpy and didn't much look like Melody Bergstrom's outline, but it would have to do. He grabbed the woman's wrist and pulled her down into the ravine as he shoved the vegetation-filled dress into her place.

"What's that?" demanded Wall. He sprang to his feet, his hand flashing to the pistol hanging at his side.

Slocum clamped his hand firmly over Melody's mouth to keep her quiet. He waited for the telltale sounds of Wall coming to investigate.

"You're gettin' spooked over nothing, Emmett," the other gunman said. "Sit down and let's finish the hand. I got you fair and square and I ain't lettin' you weasel out now."

"I got you, not the other way round."

Slocum chanced a quick look. Wall had returned to his card game. This allowed Slocum to prop up the dress and put a small bush where Melody's head ought to be. Any inspection would reveal the deception, but all it had to do was keep the men quiet for a few more minutes. Slocum would be happy with five and only Lady Luck could grant him a ten-minute head start.

He motioned to Melody Bergstrom, who tried to hold back. He snared her slender wrist and tugged her along on her belly down the arroyo's sandy bottom. When they got a ways from the camp, Slocum let her stand.

"I'm cold," she protested. The lovely woman tried to hide the places where her naked flesh poked through holes torn in her frilly undergarments.

"You'll be a sight colder if Wall has his way with you. Come on, and try not to make any noise." Slocum started back up the hill, moving as silently as a shadow slipping across another shadow. Melody Bergstrom followed almost as quietly, only an occasional grating of stone against stone betraying her passage. They got back to where Slocum's roan contentedly nibbled at the sparse grass.

"Can you ride?" he asked.

"Of course I can," she snapped. "What do you take me for, a hothouse flower?"

"Get on up. We've got to put a few miles between us and those men."

"Are we going back to the Denver and Utah camp?"

"As quick as we can," Slocum promised. This answer seemed to be the one that let the woman relax. She climbed into the saddle and didn't protest as Slocum got on behind her. If anything, she seemed to appreciate it.

They started riding, slowly at first to let the horse get used to the added weight, then faster when Slocum was sure the roan could manage the pace without stumbling. They hadn't ridden two miles when they heard gunshots from the direction of the camp where Melody had been held.

"Reckon they've discovered your sage-filled dress," Slocum said. "There's no way we can outrun them, and I don't know the trails in these mountains."

"I'm not too sure, myself," Melody said, "but we can take that path downhill a ways and hole up in an old mine shaft. The ore played out years ago."

"We can try to make your pa's camp," Slocum said.

"Too risky. I don't want Emmett Wall catching me again. You have enough ammunition to hold off a small army until daylight. By then Gus could muster enough men to come rescue us, if necessary."

"Unless Wall is one hell of a better tracker than I am, he would never find us. And how do you know how much ammo I have?"

"I felt it in your saddlebags when I mounted," she said. "I'm not stupid. Don't ever underestimate me."

"Sorry," Slocum said, guiding the roan down the steep slope. He found the dark hole of a mine without problem and rode straight into it. He had to dismount after a few yards when the roof dropped suddenly to little more than man-high.

"The horse will be just fine here for the night," Melody said. "There's a little pool of water and we can place our blankets back there."

"You sound as if you've been here before." Slocum paced around, studying the area. It was everything she claimed it was.

"I worked with my father's survey team. We spent more than one night in the area."

"Good," Slocum said, "but there's a problem. All I've got is one blanket."

Slocum found the woman standing close to him, very close. Her warm body pressed into his and her arms circled his neck. She looked up, her brown eyes locking on his green ones.

"What's the problem? There's room for both of us in that blanket, isn't there?"

Her fingers laced through his lank black hair and pulled his face to hers. She kissed him firmly. It took Slocum a few seconds to respond. He hadn't expected this from the daughter of a railroad tycoon. Fact was, he didn't know what to expect from Melody Bergstrom.

Her body rubbed against his with more insistence. When she reached down and began unfastening his gun belt, he stepped back.

"Is this smart?" he asked. "Wall might be on our trail."

"The horse will warn us. You said it yourself. Wall isn't as good a tracker as you are, is he? And you deserve a reward for risking your life for me."

Her passion surprised Slocum. She almost tore his clothing off. He moved more gently, still unsure of her. Melody wanted everything, though, and she wanted it now. Slocum barely got the blanket spread when the woman was forcing him down on it. As she moved, her undergarment parted slightly and exposed her luscious left breast. Slocum moved and caught the ruddy tip in his mouth.

He sucked hard enough to make the woman moan. Then he used his tongue to tease and torment her a little. But it was Melody who got the better of him. As his tongue danced and slid over her breast, she was reaching between his legs. She caught his turgid length and tugged hard enough on it to make him grunt.

"This is what I want, John. And you know where I want it."

"Do I?" he teased "Could it be here?" His hand stroked over the slight dome of her belly. He pushed up the cotton garment and revealed sleek thighs and a dark triangle nestled between. "Or could it be down here?"

He stroked up the inside of her legs. She shivered all over.

"Don't tease me like this. Please."

He kept up the stroking, the touching, the occasional kiss on exposed flesh until she was moaning in stark desire. Only then did he move between her spread legs and position himself. The tip of his manhood touched her nether lips.

"Now, John, yes, oh, yes!"

He didn't need Melody's urging to continue. He slipped forward, burying himself balls deep in her yearning interior. The woman shrieked in unbridled ecstasy at the intrusion. Slocum pulled back a ways until just the purpled tip of his shaft remained inside. Then he sampled the slick, hot delight of her body again.

The rhythmic motion caused his balls to tighten and threaten to explode. It had been a while since he'd been with a woman as lovely as Melody Bergstrom. And it had been even longer since he had been with one so eager for what he had to offer.

She reached up and stroked his hair, his cheeks, then moved down the sides of his moving body. She knew all the right places to touch to arouse him more. He bent down and licked at the hard pebble now capping her lustrous white breast. This caused Melody to curve her back in wanton craving for what he was giving her so freely.

As she arched up, he penetrated her even more deeply. Slocum felt her body around him, tensing in erotic frenzy. Pressure around him mounted as she rocked through tumultuous emotions. She cried out and clawed at him and urged him to move even faster.

Slocum didn't think it was possible, but he found hidden resources. He slammed repeatedly into her until the white-hot tide rose within his balls and spilled out.

Spent, he collapsed onto her. They lay together, gasping for breath and letting the cool night air evaporate the sweat on their bodies.

"You're good, John—at many things."

He rolled over and silently studied her. Melody Bergstrom was a woman of many accomplishments. He was beginning to think he had done the right thing lying about the hand Gus Maguire had dealt him. Slocum wouldn't have traded a hundred dollars in gold dust for the past few minutes.

4

Slocum stirred and then sat bolt upright when he heard a faint whistling sound outside. He blinked, rubbed the sleep from his eyes, and crawled forward in the mine. He grabbed his Winchester and then fell flat on his belly to peer out the mouth of the shaft. The land fell away abruptly just a few yards outside. Dark tailings tumbled to the valley floor below and only the barest of paths led to the mine. Slocum shivered. He was glad he hadn't seen how close to the edge the horse had been the night before. One misstep and they would have tumbled into the canyon below.

The whistling came again. Slocum moved forward a bit more and peered around the edge of the mine's rocky mouth. During the night, a shrub had broken in the wind and wedged itself into a crevice, forming a strange musical instrument. The harder the wind blew, the louder the whistling. Slocum waited a few minutes, just to be sure he was right. Seeing nothing, he retreated into the mine, patted the horse, and then climbed into his trousers.

Melody Bergstrom still slept peacefully, what little clothing she had left to her pulled up just under her chin as a blanket. Bare patches of her lustrous skin poked out here and there and caused a reaction in Slocum that he didn't much like. He ought to keep better control of himself, even when the woman was as good looking as this one. If he started thinking with his balls instead of his brains, they'd both end up dead. Emmett Wall and his henchmen weren't going to just give up on their kidnapping, not if a quarter million dollar railroad contract with the government was at stake.

Slocum settled his cross-draw holster into place and checked the load in his Colt Navy. Only then did he go exploring. Just outside the mine he saw evidence of small animals, a rabbit, maybe, and a few ground squirrels. He considered bagging several for breakfast. His belly rubbed against his spine and produced a constant low growling. If Wall wasn't around, hunting would be all right, but Slocum didn't want to bring the entire crew from the Rocky Mountain Rail Line down on them. He counted himself as being more lucky than skillful getting away as he had the night before.

A soft scraping noise behind made him spin, go into a crouch, and bring up the rifle. Melody Bergstrom centered in his sights.

"Don't go sneaking up on me like that," he said, relaxing.

"I've never seen a man with such quick reflexes," the woman said admiringly. "You *do* have many talents. Are you really working for my father?"

"Gus Maguire hired me until the track gets laid through Widowmaker Pass. I've never even seen your pa."

"He went back to Denver to arrange some financing for the railroad. He's always on the move, never stopping. It's no wonder you've never met him. It would have bothered me sorely if you'd claimed you'd seen him at the camp."

Slocum had the feeling that this would change soon enough. He turned his attention back to the terrain. The steep drop-off by the path leading into the mine showed that a larger road had existed at one time, but the rock had given way. A large wagon lay upside down in the canyon. Slocum wondered how many men had died in it.

"We don't need breakfast," Melody said. The brunette pulled the blanket around her shoulders as a gust of wind whipped down the canyon. The mournful howling sounded again where the wood vibrated against the rocky wall above them.

"But you do need some clothing. I've got a spare shirt and trousers. The fit will be poor, but it's better than riding around almost buck naked."

"Do you really think so?" she teased. Melody let the blanket slip from her bare shoulders. The merest hint of succulent breast showed itself to Slocum. As she turned, he got an even better look at forbidden parts of her anatomy. Melody looked back coquettishly and smiled at him. "Where do I find these clothes of yours?"

"Can't wait to get into my pants, is that it?" Slocum asked.

Melody laughed delightedly. She looped her arm through his as they went back into the mine. Slocum rummaged in his saddlebags until he found the tattered shirt and old canvas pants. He watched in appreciation as Melody put them on. The shirt had shrunk from too many washings and fit the woman better than it had any right to, but the pants didn't come within a country mile of fitting.

Before either could comment on it, Slocum heard rocks clattering down the side of the canyon outside. He put his index finger to his lips and cautioned her to silence. Motioning for her to prepare the horse, he went to investigate the intruders.

Slocum let out a sigh of relief when he saw Gus Maguire and a couple of the Irish workmen with him. He lifted the rifle and waved to the man making his way down the treacherous path. Slocum glanced back and was happy to see that Melody was entirely dressed now. It wouldn't do explaining what had happened in the mine. The railroad foreman seemed to take an almost paternal protective attitude toward the woman.

"Slocum, there ye be. We thought we'd plumb lost ye back there until Josh here saw the path leading to the mine. Miss Bergstrom's with ye, ain't she?"

"I am, Gus," Melody said, leading the horse from the mine. The foreman's eyes widened when he saw her wearing Slocum's clothes. "Mr. Slocum was kind enough to rescue me from those ruffians. Damn Wall, anyway!"

"We'll fix him for sure, ma'am," the one named Josh said. "We'll go ridin' into their camp and—"

"And nothing," said Slocum. "You can fight or you can lay track. Miss Bergstrom is safe and unharmed." He looked at the woman for her to verify that. She nodded, her uncombed brown hair floating on the wind and forming a small, delightful cloud around her perfect face. Melody pushed the hair back and laughed.

"He plucked me from the middle of their camp as sweet as you please, Gus. It was a sight to be seen, believe me."

"They didn't harm ye none, now did they? That Wall's a mean customer."

"Mr. Slocum would never allow that," Melody said. "I'm fine, really, none the worse for my small adventure. Has Papa returned to camp yet?"

"He's due in by midmorning." Maguire cleared his throat and looked from Slocum to Melody Bergstrom. "What are we gonna tell him about last night?"

"Why tell him anything, Gus?" Melody smiled sweetly. "He worries so about me. There's no need for him to do that any longer, don't you think?" She turned her brown eyes on Slocum. Slocum tried to read the message there and failed. It wasn't love. It wasn't admiration, but he was damned if he could say it wasn't just simple outright lust. This filly was a spirited one and knew what she wanted—and usually got it, if Slocum was any judge of character.

"You think we could keep it from him?" The foreman didn't sound convinced. "This here Wall's got to be stopped."

"You'll stop him if you beat him to the other side of the divide," Melody said. "I wasn't harmed, thanks to Mr. Slocum. Now, let's not stand around all day. I'm anxious to get back to camp."

Gus Maguire said nothing as he watched his boss's daughter climb onto her horse. The shirt and trousers she wore sparked interest in both the foreman and the others with him, but no one asked why she was wearing Slocum's old clothes.

As they rode out, Melody in the lead, Slocum spoke with Maguire. "Her dress got torn up something fierce from the fight she put up against Wall. Couldn't let her ride around in her unmentionables."

"Reckon not," Maguire said, still openly skeptical. He eyed Slocum and added, "Mr. Bergstrom's a fair man, but he don't take kindly to anyone nosin' around his only daughter."

"It'd be hard finding a man good enough for her," Slocum allowed. He knew this didn't satisfy Maguire, but he didn't much care. As far as Slocum was concerned, he'd already received his reward for rescuing Melody Bergstrom from Wall and the others. Anything he was paid from now on would be strictly for hire, cash money on the barrelhead.

They rode back to the Denver and Utah camp. Slocum hadn't seen much of Parsons's camp, but there was a feeling of excitement here that told him the workers enjoyed what they did. The Irish railroad crew worked hard and they played hard and enjoyed both equally.

"We'll get ye settled in and on the job," Maguire said, "as soon as I see to Miss Bergstrom." The foreman rode off with Melody and left Slocum to poke around the camp.

Several men remembered him from the night before and the fistfight with Emmett Wall. They cheered him and waved. The others who had ridden with Maguire quickly passed the word that Slocum had rescued their employer's daughter. This caused Slocum's stock to soar even more with the men.

When he lent a hand moving the heavy steel rails and showed he was capable of keeping pace with them at their work, he became something of a hero. Slocum toiled for more than an hour moving the track into place and letting the others swing their heavy sledgehammers, driving in the iron spikes. Only when Maguire came out and motioned to him did Slocum wipe the sweat from his face and go see what the man wanted.

"We got plenty of workers, Slocum," Maguire said. "You don't have to work out there. We want you keepin' the supplies safe from those marauding whoresons from Parsons's camp."

Slocum dusted off his dirty hands and picked up his shirt. He hadn't worked this hard in some time and it felt good. The high altitude in the Rockies tore a mite at his lungs, but this passed after a spell. He stretched and then buckled on his holster.

"Where's the supply dump?" he asked. "I'll need to reconnoiter the area to see where the best observation point is."

"Ye talk like a military man. Ye see action in the war?"

Slocum nodded but didn't elaborate. He had no desire to tell of his experiences as a sniper for the Confederacy. He'd sit on a hill waiting for the flash of sunlight off some Yank officer's gold braid. A careful sighting, a slow squeeze, and the enemy lacked a commander. It hadn't been good work, but it had been necessary, and it certainly was a sight better than riding with Quantrill and his butchers.

"I'm likin' this more and more," Maguire said, rubbing his hands together. "It surely was a stroke of luck me beatin' you in the card game the way I did. We Irish aren't used to havin' things run our way."

Slocum had noticed that the workers, happy though they seemed, tended to be a pessimistic lot. They told of wakes where they got drunk and laughed far into the night at a friend's funeral and a birthing where everyone cried in sorrow for bringing another life into the world. It seemed to Slocum they had everything backward.

Or maybe not, if your life was harsh enough.

"We're movin' good today. We got our boss's daughter back, Mr. Bergstrom is due in sometime late on this afternoon, and we'll be leavin' this camp and strikin' out for a new one yonder." Maguire pointed vaguely toward the towering peaks of the Rockies.

"That means your crew won't be able to get into Central City as easily, doesn't it?" Slocum asked.

Maguire coughed and rubbed his stubbled chin. Slocum wondered if the foreman ever tried to shave.

"You've got a good head on your shoulders, ye do, Slocum. Reckon it won't hurt ye none to watch over the boys as they make one last hoot of it?"

Slocum saw he didn't have much choice. He nodded, then turned and went off to get some rest. He was tired, and he would be even more tired before he got back to camp after nursemaiding the railroad crew.

"You're a good sport, Slocum. We like that." The man slapped Slocum so hard on the back that his teeth clacked together. Slocum had broken up four different fights and kept the men out of jail as a result. The sheriff kept poking his nose into the saloon and looking for trouble, but so far Slocum had kept it to a minimum. Clarence Bergstrom couldn't afford to lose any of his crew to a thirty day jail sentence for drunk and disorderly, and he sure as hell couldn't afford to pay a hefty fine, if the Central City judge decided to impose one.

"Where's the new camp going to be?" Slocum asked, hoping to keep the man from pounding more on him.

"Just this side of Widowmaker Pass. Once we're through there, the rest will be easy, level track-layin', a nice li'l ol' town to put up in, everything. But that pass." The man shook his shaggy head sadly. "They don't call it the Widowmaker for nothing."

"Someone's tried to put track through before?"

"Twice, and they failed. One got froze up in the middle of winter cuz they didn't work quick enough. The other tried without knowin' what the hell they was doing."

"Maguire knows what he's doing," Slocum said, not quite turning it into a question.

"Gus is the best, and we got all the support we need from Mr. Bergstrom. And that daughter of his. You seen her, Slocum. Ain't she a sight for sore eyes? And she's hotter'n a pistol, too. Let's drink to her."

Everyone in the saloon drank to Melody Bergstrom's good health. And then they all drank to Clarence Bergstrom. And to Maguire and to Slocum. After the fifth or sixth round of toasts Slocum lost track why they were drinking. And it really didn't matter. Any excuse would do.

He moved away to let his head clear. The whiskey had clouded his vision and made his head spin. He still wasn't used to the high altitude and the liquor went to his head quicker than he liked.

Outside he let the cold clear air drive away the cobwebs inside. He coughed and spat, then sat in a straight-backed wooden chair and watched the traffic in the Central City street. As he sobered up a mite, he began thinking. Only Bergstrom's men were in town. He didn't see any who might be workers for the Rocky Mountain Rail Line.

Slocum worked this over, then remembered something Melody had said about Parsons hiring Chinese. They didn't drink, and Anthony Parsons wasn't likely to let them out of camp. Only the likes of Emmett Wall were allowed into town, Slocum decided. Using the Chinese laborers had both good and bad points. The men would work until they dropped from exhaustion, ate little, and didn't cause much trouble. The downside was keeping them like slaves. Slocum doubted either Wall or Parsons worried much on this point.

He heard another fight starting inside. He heaved himself to his feet and went to see what the ruckus was about. The Irish liked their fights and didn't mean anything by them, but the sheriff didn't see it that way.

Two men—best friends from everything Slocum had seen earlier in the day—were hammering away at each other as if they were the worst enemies in the world. Both were too drunk to do any harm to the other, unless a lucky punch happened to land. Slocum waited for the men to tire themselves out a bit more, then took one out with a pistol barrel to the side of his head. Before the other could complain about the injury done his friend, Slocum turned and laid him out, too.

"Drinks are on me!" he called and the others forgot all about the fight as they went to drink up more of Slocum's hard-earned money. Still, this was the easiest way of keeping order, and Slocum didn't begrudge the men their fun. He bent and lugged one man out onto the boardwalk to let him come to slowly. Before he went back for the other man, Slocum straightened and listened hard. Another fight from the whiskey bar down the street caught his attention. He tried to remember which of Bergstrom's men weren't here and couldn't. It might mean nothing, but something gnawed away at Slocum.

He left the man snoring quietly on the walk and hurried down the street to peer into the next saloon. His heart jumped into his throat when he saw the men in the saloon.

A stocky man lay facedown on the floor, the sheriff standing over him with a shotgun aimed at the back of his head. Off in a corner, smirking, were Emmett Wall and a henchman. And sprawled across a green-topped table amid a spray of cards and poker chips lay a man with a bullet hole in the center of his head.

"What's going on, Sheriff?" Slocum asked. His heart dropped even more when the lawman answered.

"Got myself a murderer here. Caught him red-handed. Got eyewitnesses to the killing." He rolled the man over.

"This one's gonna hang for sure. Nobody goes around killing tinhorn gamblers in my town and gets away with it."

Slocum had already figured out the sheriff's prisoner was Gus Maguire.

5

"You can't let him rot in jail!" cried Melody Bergstrom. She stamped her foot and spun in tight circles like a trapped animal. "You can't do it, John. It—it's inhuman to let Gus stay in that awful jail. You saw it. That filthy cell is hardly big enough for him to lie down in."

"He's not being treated any worse than any other prisoner," Slocum said. He had almost said "any other murderer" but had caught himself. Melody was upset and had every right to be.

Slocum had asked around and had found out everything the sheriff knew of the crime. Maguire and the gambler from Kansas City had been playing cards, and Maguire had been losing steadily. Nobody mentioned that the foreman had been upset over this; Slocum had asked several of his railroad crew and they all said Maguire was a terrible card player and accepted it. What he couldn't accept was stopping his gambling. He was addicted to it, if reconciled to losing his pay week after week making wild bets in games he could never win.

Maguire hadn't been upset, but somehow a bullet had crashed through the tinhorn's head and sent him sprawling

40

over the table. There had been the commotion Slocum had heard, and then the sheriff came bursting in.

"He was framed. Gus would never kill a man like that over a poker game."

"Did Maguire wear a six-shooter?" Slocum asked. For a moment Melody let her mouth fall open. She tried to speak and couldn't find the words. She finally croaked out her answer.

"No, he didn't even own a gun. If he had one, he took it from the armory. You know where I mean, the locker in the supply car."

"We can check to see if there's a pistol missing," Slocum said.

"He didn't kill that man! He's being framed!"

"Of course he is," Slocum said. "I know who's behind it, too, but that doesn't get Maguire out of jail. We need more proof."

"But he wouldn't kill anyone, and if he did, it'd be with his bare hands. Gus was like that."

"Don't go trying to convince the sheriff," Slocum cautioned her. With Melody Bergstrom as a witness, the prosecution wouldn't even need Wall and his friend perjuring themselves. Slocum had worked to keep Maguire's crew from rushing the jail and springing their foreman. This would only have made matters worse. The sheriff was already hiring on more deputies to take care of what he thought would be a nasty situation getting Maguire to trial.

"What are you going to do? You can't let him stay there. I mean, he's a good person, but my father *needs* him. There's no way we can get the track laid through the pass without Gus."

"There are always other foremen," Slocum said.

"Such as you? Can you keep the crew working? We're not laying a narrow gage. This is a full-sized railroad. We need a good bed, one that won't give way when the first fully loaded freight train goes over the track. Can you blast away the mountain and keep the bed level and be sure the rails are tight? Gus can do all that and more and never work up a sweat."

"There's no one else you can hire?"

Melody snorted in disgust. "No one I'd trust not to be working for Parsons. He can hire away the best men and ship them off somewhere else since his labor costs are so low. He hardly feeds those Celestials working for him. A bowl of rice and they're probably happy."

"Getting fed that much will do it," Slocum said sarcastically. He understood the business end of this race. Parsons had little overhead other than the cost of the track, and if what Melody and Maguire had said was right, Parsons didn't intend keeping the line running for long after it was finished. Slipshod work was good enough for him and the trestle he was building across Grand Gorge.

"We can break him out. If we—"

"That won't work," Slocum said. "The sheriff has a small army waiting for us to try. And where would Maguire go?"

"Why, he could come back to camp and do his work and—" She bit off the sentence when she realized what he meant. Gus Maguire couldn't return to the Denver and Utah camp without the sheriff tracking him down easily. "What do you suggest we do?"

"I don't like it, but he's got to stay put for a while. I need time to find out who actually pulled the trigger. That's about all the sheriff's going to listen to."

"He's been bought by Parsons. Why do you think he'll be amenable to jailing someone else for the crime?" Melody was still furious. Slocum saw how the color had rushed into the woman's cheeks and made her even more beautiful than before.

"I've asked around. The sheriff's not in Parsons's hip pocket, no matter what you think. He's doing his job by putting Maguire in jail. And he'll do his job when I find the real murderer."

"Just like that he'll let Gus go?" Melody snapped her fingers.

Slocum nodded. He had to believe it. There didn't seem to be any other course of action. Standing around jawing about the murder wasn't doing anyone any good, either. He had to get on it, and he knew where to start.

"I'm coming with you," Melody said suddenly. "Gus is my friend. He's risked his life for me. I want to help."

Slocum started to argue, then stopped and thought it over. Part of his job was looking after Melody Bergstrom. He couldn't do it if he went out on the killer's trail, and this meant she was vulnerable to Emmett Wall's kidnapping attempts again. On the other hand, if she rode with him, he'd be able to keep an eye on her and get a line on the man who had framed Gus Maguire.

"All right," he said. From the expression on her face Slocum knew he had surprised her. The lovely brunette had thought she would have to argue the point.

"Let's get started, then," she said. "Where do we go first?"

"The saloon," Slocum said. "I've already talked to the barkeep and got an idea what happened. I want to be sure it happened the way I think."

There was quite a stir in the saloon when Slocum and Melody walked in. Women weren't usually patrons of a saloon, and especially not proper young ladies like Melody Bergstrom. The barkeep looked uneasy and motioned to Slocum.

"She ain't supposed to be in here. I mean, she's not *that* kind of woman."

"You mean I do not look like a soiled dove?" Melody said loud enough for the others in the saloon to hear. "I assure you I am not a Cyprian lady."

"Didn't think so, but—"

"We'll be just a minute or two," Slocum said. The barkeep looked uneasy, then moved away to talk with several men at the far end of the bar. Slocum turned to Melody and said, "Let's make this quick. One of those owlhoots is going to come over and make trouble in a minute or two, when he works up enough nerve."

"What do you need me to do, John?"

"Sit there where the dead man was, facing the door. Yes, right there." Slocum moved quickly to the swinging doors leading into the saloon. He peered over the top of the wood doors, then studied them. He smiled crookedly when he saw the splinter knocked from the top of the door where the murderer's barrel had rested. The cowboy had been shot from outside. In the confusion following the death, Wall had dropped a six-shooter under the table to make it seem that Gus Maguire had committed the crime.

Slocum motioned to Melody to leave. The others at the bar relaxed a mite at having a decent woman out of the saloon. They were used to whores working the cribs out back, and now and then there might be a traveling troupe with shameless women doing racy French dances, but the likes of Melody Bergstrom were never seen within these walls.

"What have you discovered, John?"

"The killer rested his rifle here." Slocum stopped and thought on this. Rifle. The killer had used a rifle. He dropped to his knees and looked around until he found a spent .44-40 brass cartridge. Picking it up, he stared at it.

"This is enough to get Gus out of jail, then," Melody said. "He couldn't stand out here on the boardwalk and fire and be at the table at the same time."

"It doesn't prove anything, but we're getting there. All we have to do is find the rifle this was fired from and we have the murderer."

"But Gus—"

"Will have to stay in jail for a spell longer," Slocum said. Something bothered him, but he couldn't put his finger on it. Melody was almost right that this was evidence enough to get Maguire out, but he couldn't rightly say why. No matter what, it would be better bringing the killer to justice.

That made life easier for the sheriff and made him more inclined to let Maguire out.

Slocum circled the saloon, paying attention to the dusty ground. He found where a horse had been tethered. It meant little, but why bother keeping a horse at the side of the saloon when it was just as easy to tie it up in front near a watering trough? He walked a ways and saw the direction taken. The tracks got jumbled with dozens of other animals but Slocum knew the direction and it was straight out of town.

"Let's ride," he said. He held back a deep yawn. He hadn't gotten any sleep the night before, and now the first fingers of dawn were stroking the eastern sky, turning it from gray to pink with bits of blue all around. It would be a beautiful fall day in Colorado—if he could find the gambler's killer.

"That way?" asked Melody.

"Reckon so. Why?"

"That's the direction of the Rocky Mountain Rail Line Camp. Those cayuses won't let us just ride on in and take one of their men."

"That's why I'm hoping we can overtake him."

"But the killing was hours ago. How can you hope to?"

"I figure he laid low for a spell after Wall planted the gun under the table. He didn't want to be obvious about leaving town in a hurry. And there's something else. From the tracks, I think his horse was about to throw a shoe. He might be walking a lame animal back into the camp."

"Hurry, John, we can do it. We can get him before he joins up with Wall again." Melody put her heels into her horse's sides and shot off. Slocum was slower to follow, not wanting to tire his roan early in the chase. He saw evidence of the loose shoe, but if it hadn't come off, the man was already back in the enemy camp.

He caught up with Melody when her horse began to tire from the frantic pace. He let the roan have its head, and he occasionally dropped to the ground to check the trail. He found enough spoor to convince him they were still on the right track.

"What about the horse going lame? Did it?" she demanded.

Slocum looked up from where he had dropped to one knee to study the trail. He ran his hand through the dust and came up with a horseshoe. Shiny bright nails stuck in the shoe showed where it had recently been nailed to a hoof.

"This is what I've been looking for," he said. "There seems to be two trails from here on, one a limping horse and the other a man on foot." Slocum outlined the boot print in the dust for Melody.

"That's amazing. I could never tell that's what it was."

"I've had practice tracking," Slocum said, puffing up a little from the woman's compliment. "And I knew what I was looking for. Now's the time to really ride. I want him before he gets too close to the construction site."

"It's only a few miles more on down the road," Melody said. She showed a tad of nervousness at going back to where Wall and the others had held her prisoner, but for Gus Maguire she'd ride through hell. Slocum appreciated the woman's loyalty. Maguire had to be a special person to deserve such courage on Melody's part.

They rode in silence until they came to the top of a rise. The road curled down and to the west toward Parsons's construction site. In the distance, Slocum saw the wooden trestle slowly spanning the Grand Gorge. Work was almost half done on it and, from the way dozens of Celestials bustled around, it wouldn't take more than a week to finish the rest. Once this was done, Anthony Parsons would have won. The rest of his track would be easy to lay and Bergstrom still had to fight his way across the entire stretch of Widowmaker Pass.

"There, John, there's a man walking his horse. See?"

Slocum stood in his stirrups and peered down the road. He saw the small dust cloud being kicked up, and he knew they were too late. The man was being greeted by Emmett Wall and the other gunmen Parsons's foreman had hired. Getting the culprit out of the camp would take the entire U.S. Army Cavalry, and Slocum didn't think they'd be amenable to the chore.

6

"Well, what are you waiting for?" Melody Bergstrom turned to Slocum and looked angry that he wasn't rushing headlong into Parsons's camp to retrieve the murderer.

"What do you want me to do?" Slocum asked. "I can't fight off Wall and all the others."

"So you're just giving up?"

"No," Slocum said slowly. He studied the area and saw a dozen different places to watch the construction camp. Sooner or later the killer would leave, and when he did, Slocum would have to act quickly. But it would be stealth and not bravado that won the day.

"Mr. Slocum, what are you going to do?" Melody was so distressed at his lack of action that she called him mister rather than by his Christian name. He thought this was a bit funny considering that the night they had spent together had been uninhibited and one totally lacking in formality between them.

"First off, getting myself killed isn't going to help Maguire. Until that owlhoot rides out of camp alone there's not much chance of capturing him. We're going to sit on a hill and just wait."

"That's all?"

"Unless you can suggest something else. Want to go back to camp and get all the workers to make an attack on Parsons? I reckon we'd take upward of fifty percent casualties."

"What do you mean? That Wall and his men would kill half our crew?"

"Easily," Slocum said. "That camp is more easily defensible than it looks at first glance. You've got to ride between those hills to get there, and two men with rifles could hold off a small army. Parsons gets most of his supplies on the rail line he's already laid. That might be a way into camp, but they watch the trains coming in real close. I don't see any way of forcing the killer out."

"Do you know which man it is? I never got a look at his face."

"Reckon so," Slocum said. He had seen the flash of sunlight off a big silver belt buckle. There couldn't be too many men in a working camp with a buckle like that. And a red-and-white bandanna added a bit more in the way of identification. It wasn't much, but it'd have to be enough.

"So we just watch?"

"From over there," Slocum said, pointing to a spot on another rise. "We can see the camp and watch the comings and goings. And there's something you've got to take care of."

"What's that?"

Slocum pointed to the silver conch belt the woman wore. He reached into his shirt pocket and pulled out the two hand-tooled conches that she had dropped during her kidnapping and handed them to her.

"Where? Oh, from before." Melody shivered. "I suppose I ought to take off the belt, too. We wouldn't want sunlight shining off it, would we?"

Slocum watched as she unlooped the silver from around her waist and stashed it in her saddlebags. Every movement was liquid and graceful and reminded Slocum of the night they'd spent so pleasurably. He wished they could find a secluded spot to while away what he knew would be long hours waiting for the killer in Parsons's camp, but that would be too reckless. These hills were patrolled by Wall and his gunmen, and he had to stay alert for them.

They left the road and made their way up the steeper slope. Slocum occasionally looked back down at the camp for some sign that they'd been seen. It was too early in the day for the men to be vigilant. Slocum suspected they were sitting around drinking coffee and congratulating themselves on how they had framed Gus Maguire. Slocum touched the brass cartridge he had found outside the saloon. A rifle had been used or the brass wouldn't have been there; if a Colt Peacemaker had been the murder weapon the spent brass would still be in the cylinder.

Something about this kept clawing at Slocum's brain, but he pushed it away. He had to watch and wait and nothing more. Any flight of fancy might distract him and get both him and Melody killed.

"Is this all right for our camp?" she asked, indicating a spot just over the top of the rise. "We can sit on top and not risk our horses being seen. We ought to be able to get down to the road in a hurry, when the time comes."

"You might think on going back to the Denver and Utah camp," Slocum said. "This is going to be a boring watch, and when trouble comes, it'll be fast as a bullet. Part of the reason Maguire hired me was to look after you."

"I can look after myself, thank you," she said almost primly. Melody Bergstrom stood as if a ramrod had been shoved up her spine. "Aside from the other night, I have been quite capable of keeping my own affairs in order."

"I just bet that's so," Slocum said. Again he got the feeling this was one proud woman who always got what she set her sights on.

"I will not shirk my responsibility toward Gus, either. If staying here helps him clear his name, then so be it." She sat and just stared at the Rocky Mountain Rail camp and the bustle of increasing activity among the workers.

Slocum studied the camp and made small replicas of it in the dirt at his feet. He saw how the timbers were pulled over toward the trestle and where the rail line came in from Denver with supplies for the camp. Most of all, he figured out where Emmett Wall and the others bivouacked. This reinforced his notion that getting the killer out of camp by any frontal attack was well nigh impossible. Only patience would pry him loose from this well-protected area.

"I can always sneak in when it gets dark," Slocum said, thinking aloud. "That would be dangerous, though, because getting him away without raising a ruckus would be hard."

"I wish we had a telescope with us," Melody said. "I could use the time to study how they're building that bridge. It doesn't look too sturdy to me. Not enough support beams. You might know Anthony Parsons would cut corners everywhere."

Slocum remembered what Maguire had said about Parsons intending to take the government's money and let the bridge collapse. This wasn't a business for Parsons, it was a scam. Build everything as cheaply as possible, take the reward, and then vanish. It would leave him a rich man and the towns on the far side of the divide without reliable railroad service for years to come.

"Do you figure Wall would let just anybody shoot the gambler? Or do you think the killer might be his right-hand man?"

"What? I don't know. I suppose he would use someone he trusted. What's that got to do with anything, John?"

"It gives me a place to start looking when I go down there."

"But you said—"

"When it gets dark, I'll sneak into camp. There are several places where their sentries don't patrol. We've been waiting for an hour and there's nothing but business as usual there. We might be waiting a long time. Parsons is pushing hard to finish that trestle. If the killer is Wall's crony, he might not leave camp again until the bridge is completed." Slocum didn't add, "Or when Gus Maguire is hanged."

"You're going in at sunset? What do you want me to do?"

"Stay close to the road. When I come out, there'll be a swarm of hornets on my tail." Slocum leaned back and covered his eyes with his hat. Melody watched the camp now with more interest than he could muster. He had to rest to be sharp for the attack at sundown. He drifted to sleep, only to come awake, six-shooter in his hand, when a light touch came to his shoulder. Slocum saw that Melody had let him sleep and had only awakened him when the autumn sun dipped behind the tall peaks to the west.

"I didn't know when you wanted to go," she said.

He looked around, checked his pistol, replaced it in his holster, and got to his feet. "Now's as good a time as any. I'll go in on foot. You be waiting where we first saw the camp. The horses are rested and ready to run. If I get back, we're going to need every bit of speed they can give us."

"If, John? Did you say if?"

He turned and saw her brown eyes glistening in the last rays of the sun. Tears formed at the corners of her eyes.

"When," he corrected. Slocum wanted to put as good a face on it as possible for her, but he couldn't fool himself. He was walking into the jaws of a powerful trap and might not be able to wiggle free.

"I don't want to lose you, too. First Gus and then you. I couldn't bear that. Come back, John, come back to me."

He wasn't sure if she was asking him to forget the foray and let Maguire rot in jail or if she just wanted to give him additional incentive to return. It didn't matter. He bent and kissed her upturned lips. She shivered lightly and clung tightly to him.

"You *will* come back, won't you?"

"Don't figure to get myself killed, not yet at any rate," he said. Slocum held her close for a moment and felt the hurried beating of her heart, then pushed her away. He had a long way to walk just to reach the camp.

"I'll be waiting with the horses," Melody promised. Slocum nodded, turned, and left without saying anything more. He didn't quite trust himself. And what was there to say to the woman that hadn't already been said with their parting kiss? As he walked, Slocum tried to figure out why he was doing this. For Maguire? He liked the hairy old galoot, but that was hardly reason to get himself killed. For Melody? Thinking with his balls rather than his brain was a good way to get in a peck of trouble. So why was he going after the cowboy's killer?

Slocum worked on that answer as he neared the railroad camp. It finally came down to him not much liking Emmett Wall and the way the man's mustache twitched. Slocum didn't cotton to the idea of Wall framing Maguire for murder or much of anything else the man did. Kidnapping women and all the rest of Wall's doings rankled like a nettle under a saddle blanket. This was one way Slocum had of getting back at the foreman.

He slipped into camp, boldly walking past the sentry who smoked a hand-rolled cigarette. The guard never even looked up as Slocum entered the camp and made straight for Wall's tent.

Not sure who he was looking for and where to find him, Slocum decided being bold was the only way to go. He poked his head into Wall's tent, but the foreman wasn't inside. Slocum almost spun and drew his pistol when a voice from behind said, "Wall's not in. He and Jacobs are out checkin' the trestle."

"Thanks. Guess I'll go look for 'em at the gorge."

Slocum turned slowly and watched as the guard sauntered off, unaware that he had been talking to an intruder. Slocum relaxed and went into the tent, rummaging through Wall's belongings looking for something to clear Maguire. He stopped and scratched his head. Then a slow smile crossed his lips. He knew what it was that had been bothering him, and knew how they could clear Gus Maguire, even if he wasn't able to get the real killer back to Central City.

Slocum quickly left the tent, but instead of returning to where Melody waited for him, he turned toward the bridge almost spanning Grand Gorge. He could prove Maguire was innocent of the shooting, but it would be better to have a confession from the real killer. With any luck, the confession might also implicate Emmett Wall. Anything that slowed Parsons's building would be recompense enough for the time Maguire had already spent in jail.

He walked through the camp, staying in shadows and trying not to engage in conversation. By the time he reached the bivouac for the Chinese laborers, he knew he was past being found out. The Celestials watched him with dark eyes, their faces masks that hid their emotions. Slocum wondered what they felt about being exploited to build the railroad. They had to care, but he wasn't going to try to organize them into a strike against Anthony Parsons.

"Up there," shouted Wall. "See where they've been screwin' it all up?"

"Yeah, Emmett, I see it. What you want me to do?"

"Hell, Jacobs, I'm payin' you good money to make it right. You figure out what it'll take to put it right, then get it done. Parsons won't tolerate another day's delay in buildin' this damn bridge."

Slocum didn't hear Jacobs's reply. The man on the trestle grumbled and knelt, fiddling with something on the side of the bridge. Splinters came free and Jacobs threw a loose plank into the canyon five hundred feet below. Slocum touched the ebony handle of his Colt Navy. The time was ripe for what had to be done. Wall had returned to the camp. It wouldn't take him long to see that someone had ransacked his tent. When he did, all hell would be out for lunch.

By then Slocum intended to have a mile or more between him and the camp, and Jacobs would be with him, ready to confess to a murder.

Slocum walked slowly out on the rickety bridge. Even in the still of the evening, the trestle didn't seem steady. His weight made it sway slightly. Running a fully loaded train, even a narrow gage, across it would be risky.

"I think I got it figured out, Emmett," Jacobs said. "All they got to do is put a few cross-timbers up and—" He turned and looked down the barrel of Slocum's Colt.

Jacobs's eyes widened and he stood slowly, his hands reaching for the sky of their own volition.

"Let's not make this any messier than it has to be," Slocum said. "I know you killed the gambler back in Central City and framed Maguire. We're going back to town and you're going to confess."

"If I don't want to do that?" Jacobs moved a little to get his hand closer to his six-shooter. Slocum cocked his Colt and aimed it squarely for the man's eyes.

"Throw your hogleg into the canyon. If it looks like you're going to make a play for me, you're buzzard bait before you hit the bottom."

Jacobs swallowed hard and did as Slocum ordered. His six-shooter tumbled over and over into the darkness. It startled both of them when it hit the ground five hundred feet below and discharged.

"Move," Slocum said, motioning for Jacobs to go past him and toward the camp. "One peep out of you and I'll cut you in half."

"You can't get away with this. Emmett'll stop you. The whole damned camp will!"

"Shut up."

Slocum was one giant raw nerve ending. Every sound, every small motion made him start. Slocum actually thought they were going to get out of camp until Wall called out to Jacobs.

Then the lead started flying.

7

Slocum didn't know who started firing. All that mattered was keeping his hide in one piece. He squeezed off a shot that took Jacobs high in the shoulder and sent him spinning to the ground. When the man tried to stand, Slocum shot him in the leg, barely grazing him. He didn't want the killer getting to safety in the camp. Then Slocum concentrated on the fusillade ripping through the air over his head.

Ducking, Slocum fired twice quickly, one shot wounding a man with a carbine. The other shot went wild but had the desired effect. Where a half dozen men had been firing at him, now they all dived for cover, not knowing what they faced in the darkness. Slocum knocked the hot cylinder from his Colt Navy and groped in his pocket for another. He fitted it in and had six more rounds ready to fire by the time Jacobs struggled to sit upright in the dust.

"To the corral or you're dead here and now," Slocum said.

"I can't ride like this!" Blood oozed between Jacobs's fingers, showing where Slocum had plugged the man in the leg. The hole in his shoulder didn't seem to bother him. Slocum decided that shock might have dulled Jacobs's senses just a mite. The pair of them didn't have the time to stand around and talk, though. An incautious rifleman poked his head up not five yards away. Slocum took the man's hat off and sent him scurrying for cover again.

"There's a whole damned army of 'em, Wall," called out the man who'd lost his hat. "Get help!"

"There's only one of them," Wall snapped. "Don't be such cowards." He stood and started toward the corral where Jacobs hobbled along trying to get to a horse. The animals bucked and snorted, milling in fright.

Slocum sighted carefully and got off a shot at the mustachioed foreman. He saw the man jerk around but didn't know if he had hit him or merely startled him. In the dim light it was hard finding a good target. Slocum aimed at a couple tongues of flame lancing out from the muzzles of six-shooters. He didn't do much more than drive the sharpshooters back for cover, but right now he was playing for time. He had to get Jacobs on a horse, and he had to get out of the camp. Sooner or later even the worst shot got lucky.

"Dammit, get your asses over here. I want him stopped!" raged Wall.

Slocum fired twice more at the foreman, trying to kill him or at least make him dive for cover.

"I don't wanna do this," protested Jacobs.

Slocum spun and pointed his Colt straight at the man's face. The coldness in his eyes told Jacobs that he was dead if he didn't obey.

"Why are you doin' this to me? What do you want from me? Wall's the foreman. Go get him."

Slocum used his last rounds to drive the gunmen to cover. He popped out the cylinder and snapped the last fully loaded one into his Colt Navy. He had six shots left and that was it. He wouldn't have time to reload the percussion cap pistol, even if he had brought the ammunition along with him.

A bullet ripped through the brim of his hat. Another kissed his cheek and brought forth a sluggish flow of blood. Slocum ignored the slight pain and held his fear in check. He had been in worse positions and gotten out alive.

He vaulted bareback onto the nearest horse in the corral. He spooked the others and got them to crash through the gate. The sudden rush of horseflesh confused his attackers and carried Jacobs with them. Slocum bent low, gripped hard with his knees and got off a couple more rounds, hitting nothing, as he rode through the camp.

He saved the remaining four rounds for Jacobs, if he needed them to keep the man in line. It would be a few minutes of hard riding before they reached the spot where Melody Bergstrom waited.

"Don't do this, mister. I ain't done nothing!"

"Shut up and ride, Jacobs," snapped Slocum. He ducked low when a few more leaden insects blindly whipped past him. Only when their whine and the report from the rifles died did Slocum pull himself upright, and it was just in time. Jacobs tried to make his bid for freedom.

Slocum got off another shot, this one taking Jacobs in the middle of the back. The man threw up his arms and went as limp as a child's rag doll. He fell from his horse and crashed hard to the ground.

Slocum tugged on his horse's mane and stopped its head-long flight. He hit the ground running and pulled Jacobs up and tossed him over the pony's bare back. Only then did he mount and urge the horse on. From the direction of the camp, he heard Wall's harsh voice trying to restore order. There wasn't much time left.

"John!" came the call. "Over here. I didn't know if you'd need help." He turned and saw Melody not twenty yards distant. She led his roan by its reins, and she had his Winchester resting across her saddle in front of her, ready to use it.

"I had to shoot him up a mite," Slocum said. "I'm not sure what condition he's in. His name's Jacobs. Does he look familiar?"

"I've seen him around," she admitted. "I can't say if he's Wall's assistant. What are we going to do?" Sounds from the camp told Slocum pursuit was imminent. Wall had regained the upper hand with his frightened men.

"There's nothing we can do but ride like the wind for Central City. Try to keep him over his horse." Slocum reached over and took the Winchester from Melody. "I'll give 'em reason to reconsider coming after us."

"What if he tries to get away?" she asked, staring at Jacobs's still form.

"Don't worry about that as much as him dying before you get there. Now ride!"

He jumped over to his roan and settled himself in the saddle. He didn't mind riding bareback, but the saddle was more comfortable and gave better support for what he wanted to do. He got his feet into the stirrups, hefted the rifle, and waited. He heard Melody riding off as he'd told her and didn't bother watching her slender form. There'd be time for that later. Right now he had some serious shooting to do.

Emmett Wall rode hell-bent for leather straight into Slocum's sights. A quick shot took the foreman from the saddle. Slocum didn't have a good feel for the shot. It hadn't killed the foreman; it might not even have wounded him seriously. Slocum pushed that from his mind and chambered another round. His roan shifted nervously under him, but he kept it under control. More shots followed the first. Slocum was sure he hit another of Parsons's henchmen, maybe killing him. The other rounds just spread terror among the already frightened men. Wall knew what they were up against, but the rest thought they faced a small army.

Slocum kept them guessing and drove them off the road to seek cover. Only then did he turn and gallop off to catch up with Melody and their prisoner.

It had been a hell of a night so far and it wasn't going to let up any.

• • •

"The doc says it don't look good." Sheriff Lake shook his head. "He does say Jacobs confessed to shooting the gambler in the Emporium Saloon earlier on. Reckon that means Maguire is free to go."

"What's wrong, Sheriff? You don't seem happy about it." Melody Bergstrom pushed close to the lawman and set her jaw. "Has Anthony Parsons paid you off to shut us down?"

"Nothing like that, Miss Bergstrom," Lake said. "There's just a matter of evidence. The six-shooter was found under the table, right there by your foreman's hand."

"We've told you what really happened, Sheriff," Slocum said. "I found this outside on the walk." He dropped the .44-40 cartridge on the table. "Jacobs used his rifle."

"Don't prove much. The cartridge could have been there for days and days, though it looks shiny enough."

"What caliber was the pistol you think Maguire used?" Slocum asked.

"What? Don't rightly know. Let's see." Sheriff Lake went to a cabinet and took out a handgun. He looked at it and shook his head. "I must be gettin' old. This here's a .32 and I'm sure the slug we took out of the gambler was bigger."

"About the size of a .44-40," Slocum finished for him.

"Could be. Looks like I was wrong all around about Gus. Makes me feel good. Really, Miss Bergstrom, I like him, and it didn't set well with me puttin' him on ice like this."

"Show how much you like him, then," she said. "Release him immediately."

Lake almost laughed. "I am gettin' old. Forgot all about that." He grabbed a ring of keys and went into the back to let Gus Maguire out of the cell. The foreman came out looking shaggier than ever and slightly confused.

"The sheriff is sayin' I am free as a bird. What's been happenin'?"

"Slocum and Miss Bergstrom found the responsible party what shot the tinhorn. He was one of Emmett Wall's men."

"I knew it!" cried Maguire. "Wall came over and dropped the gun. That's what I been tellin' you, Sheriff."

"What's this about? Heard someone usin' my name." Emmett Wall and two of his gunmen pushed their way into the crowded sheriff's office. Wall's hand rested on his six-shooter.

"We don't want any trouble, Wall," said Lake. The sheriff moved around his desk and sat down, hiking his feet to the top. Slocum thought he was getting ready to turn them over to Wall when he saw the sheriff reach down and heft a Greener goose gun and rest it on his leg. If he opened up with that, there wouldn't be anything left of Wall or his two cohorts.

"Don't go gettin' antsy, Sheriff," said Wall. "We had a bit of commotion out at the camp and we rode in to see what could be done about it."

"I heard about some of it," the sheriff said. "Seems your right-hand man killed a tinhorn gambler earlier, and it looks as if you might have been in cahoots with him. You want to talk a spell about that?"

"I don't know what you're getting at," Wall said, his eyes still on the shotgun. "Me and the boys just rode in to complain about Slocum shootin' up our camp."

"Seems he shot up Jacobs, too," Lake said, "but that's all right 'cuz Jacobs was a murderer."

"Was? He's dead?" Wall's mustache twitched as he glared at Slocum. Slocum's cold gaze never wavered.

"Deader than a doornail," Lake said. "I reckon we're gonna be talkin' a bit more about this when I get it all sorted out in my head. Don't go anywhere, Wall. There'll be a passel of questions later on. You get my drift?" Sheriff Lake held up the shotgun so Wall was staring directly down the huge bore.

The foreman glared at the sheriff, spun, and stalked from the room. His henchmen followed quickly.

"Didn't go very far in winnin' a friend in Mr. Wall," observed Maguire, working to keep from chuckling. "He's one mean sidewinder. You watch your back, Sheriff."

Lake shrugged it off. He had seen too many gunslicks through the town to get upset over a railroad foreman.

"I'll stand you a drink, Slocum," Maguire said. "I'd offer you one, too, Miss Bergstrom, but—"

"That's all right, Gus. I need to see to a line of credit at the general store. You can find me there when you're done." She batted her eyelashes in Slocum's direction and the sly smile told him he might get a reward far beyond anything he'd dreamed of when he took the job with the Denver and Utah Railroad. Melody left, Slocum watching the way her rump turned little circles in the tight jeans she wore.

"I can use a drink," Slocum said. He tried to remember when he'd eaten, much less had a good drink. He decided there had been more whiskey than food of late, but he wasn't going to turn down the offer.

"I surely do appreciate all you've done, Slocum," Maguire said. "I owe you."

"Just doing the job you hired me to do," Slocum said.

"I can see Melody's taken quite a shine to ye," the foreman said, giving Slocum a sidelong look. "Ye be careful with her, ye hear?"

Slocum didn't answer as they went into the saloon. For a moment there was silence, then a roar went up that lifted the rafters. It took better than twenty minutes before Maguire had finished explaining what had happened and how Slocum and Melody Bergstrom had rescued him.

Maguire knocked back a long drink and then said, "Best to go and relieve myself. The pressure's gettin' to be too much for an old man like me."

Slocum watched as Maguire weaved through the room, heading for the back door that led to the outhouse. As Maguire opened the rear door, Slocum looked past and got a glimpse of Emmett Wall standing near the outhouse. Slocum vaulted the bar to avoid having to push his way through the drunken Irishmen and hurried to the door, hand resting on his ebony-handled Colt Navy.

He carefully pushed open the door and peered out, not sure what he'd see. Wall might want revenge on Maguire. If so, there was no telling what he might do.

Slocum heard Wall say, "It's not that much I'm askin' of you, Gus. For a hundred dollars in gold, all you have to do is slow down the work across the pass. What do you say?"

Slocum didn't catch Gus Maguire's reply. A roar went up inside the saloon drowning out any chance of hearing. He went through the door, but by the time he was halfway to the outhouse, Wall was gone and Maguire was tending to his business.

A hundred dollars was a powerful sum of money to offer a man making less than half that a month. And all Maguire had to do was slow up laying the track across the treacherous Widowmaker Pass.

Maguire came down the path and called to Slocum, "I'll have another round waitin' for ye when ye finish, laddy buck. This is one fine night, it is, it is!"

Slocum watched Maguire enter the saloon, wondering just how fine a night it was for the foreman.

8

"Is there something wrong, John?" asked Melody Bergstrom.

Slocum swung around, trying not to look guilty. He had been watching as Gus Maguire prepared the steam engine and four freight cars for the trek up the slope of the mountain toward Widowmaker Pass. The heavy load of rail and spike, tools and equipment needed to blast and cut through the heavy granite of the Rockies to reach the other side had to be carefully stored or everything would be lost down a five hundred foot canyon. Since Slocum had heard Emmett Wall offer the money outside the saloon, he had been looking for some tiny sign of dereliction of duty on Maguire's part. That much money could be a powerful incentive to a man who lived poor and worked hard.

"Nothing's wrong," he lied.

"You've been keeping such an eagle eye on Gus that you must think something is wrong. Is Parsons likely to try to kill him? Without our foreman, Papa could never get over the pass. Gus is the most experienced and knowledgeable of any of the men working for us. He's irreplaceable to the Denver and Utah."

Slocum nodded. That was the way he saw it, too, and if Maguire was working slower than he had to, that meant the Denver and Utah might not finish before Parsons's railroad.

"I know Gus hired you to keep an eye on me," she said, batting her long dark eyelashes and fixing her brown eyes on him, "but I can take care of myself. I think Gus is a more likely target after Wall tried framing him like that back in Central City."

"We won't be heading back into town for a spell, will we?"

Melody shook her head. In spite of his worries, Slocum was captivated by the swirl of her soft chestnut hair in a cloud around her perfectly formed face. He might have seen a more beautiful woman, but he couldn't quite remember when or where. Melody Bergstrom's spell on him was enough to make him want to stick with this job until her pa's railroad got over Widowmaker Pass.

"The crew's going to be getting edgy, then," Slocum said. "They'll take watching."

"We won't be completely cut off. Look, there!" Melody squealed with joy when she saw a tall white plume of steam poke up behind a rise. "Papa's bringing in supplies from Denver. This will keep the men in camp and happy." She smiled wryly. "It'll also keep them more than a mite drunk. He's got fifteen kegs of fine Kentucky whiskey in the supplies."

Slocum followed as Melody rushed to the temporary railhead. The engine ground to a halt. The smell of hot steel filled his nostrils and flying cinders caused him to avert his face. Slocum preferred the cleaner odor of horses and growing things, but he had to admit the sight of the train was impressive. Unlike Parsons, Clarence Bergstrom had decided to run a full-width track across the continental divide to the town of Cameron. The steam engine was a full-scale 2-2-8 and powerful, easily pulling a long string of loaded freight cars over the pass when the track got laid.

Slocum looked around to check Gus Maguire's progress in getting the other train sent on its way. The foreman didn't even appear to notice the arrival of the new supplies. He yelled and waved and shouted to the engineer of the other train to pull out.

"Is there anything on this train Maguire'd need up the slope?"

"I reckon so. Food, other supplies—and the whiskey, of course." Melody hardly seemed to notice the other train pulling out. Slocum wondered how they could be so totally unaware of what happened in other parts of the small camp. She didn't notice Maguire and Maguire didn't see the new train pulling in.

A tall, heavyset man swung down from the first car. Although he dressed in rough clothing, there was an air of command and money about him that Slocum recognized instantly. He didn't have to be told this was Melody's father.

"Papa!" she cried, running to the man. She threw her arms around his neck and pulled him down for a kiss, which seemed to annoy him.

"Melody, please, there's work to be done. The freight's got to be unloaded and the train sent back for more rail before sundown, if we intend to finish this project before winter storms move in."

"You usually aren't this rushed, Papa. What's wrong?"

"They're predicting a heavy snowfall in the next few weeks."

"Who might that be, Mr. Bergstrom?" asked Slocum. "Can't rightly say I ever saw anyone who could make a decent prediction on the weather." Slocum shivered a mite when a cold blast raked down off the tall mountain peaks to the west.

"It's that damned publication. *The Old Farmer's Almanac,* they call it. Everyone says they've been remarkably accurate in their predictions for well nigh a hundred years, and the book says there'll be new snow on the ground within three weeks. And a major storm to follow within another week."

"So you're going to try to get through Widowmaker Pass in just three weeks." Slocum scratched his head. It didn't seem possible from all he'd been told about the pass.

"We can do it. We'll be following the same route another railroad tried last year. We won't have to blast as much as our original route and this might speed up our track-laying by a week or more." Clarence Bergstrom eyed Slocum, then thrust out his hand. "I reckon you're the man my Melody's been telling me so much about."

"How's that, sir?" Slocum was puzzled. Bergstrom had been in camp when he was hired on by Maguire but had left almost immediately to fetch this load of supplies. As far as he could tell, Melody hadn't been in touch with her father.

"My little girl uses the telegraph like some people breathe. It's a good thing there's no way of talking direct. She'd bankrupt this company in nothing flat with her messages once she got talking."

"Oh, Papa," said Melody. "Really, John, I just send a few telegrams to let him know what's happening."

Bergstrom reached into his pocket and pulled out a sheaf of filmy yellow sheets. "This is the 'few telegrams' she's talking about. Damned near ten of them over the past two days. I'm glad we're moving on into the mountains and away from the Central City telegraph."

"We'll be stringing our own telegraph line as we go," Slocum said, remembering that he had seen telegraph poles and several large rolls of copper wire.

"Hush, son," cautioned Bergstrom. "I didn't want Melody knowing that." He laughed and slapped Slocum on the back. "She thinks highly of you, almost as much as she does of Gus Maguire."

"High praise," Slocum said, worrying again about the foreman. He wished he could have heard what Maguire had told Wall about the bribe. If he had known Maguire better, he might have confronted the man, but Slocum wasn't sure if he could tell if the foreman was lying. Some men could hide a thing like that. Those were the men Slocum hated to play poker against. Maguire was a self-professed bad poker player, but this might have been a lie. Slocum just didn't know. Better to watch and wait and see if the foreman did anything out of the ordinary to slow work than to accuse him openly. The worst of it was that he liked the man and hated himself for being so suspicious.

"That it is," said Bergstrom. "Get the men unloading this, will you, Slocum? I want to talk with Gus."

"He's on the train going up the grade toward the pass," Slocum said. "The freight train just pulled out."

"Damnation, I always seem to be missing my appointments. Can't make anything work since your mother died," he said, talking more to Melody and himself than to Slocum.

The railroad magnate and his daughter walked away, leaving Slocum the chore of organizing men into a crew. His position in the camp was uncertain, but the men jumped to the work fast enough. Slocum was careful to do his share of the heavy work. He wasn't a foreman; he didn't have any fancy title to get the men to work with him. The best he could do was win some measure of their respect.

When the freight train's contents were stacked along the track, the engineer blew the whistle, began backing up, and within ten minutes was out of sight.

"He gonna run that damned train backward all the way to Denver?" asked one of the roustabouts.

"Reckon he's got a turnaround somewhere between here and there," Slocum said. "And I reckon Maguire will eat your liver for breakfast if you don't have everything ready to load up when he gets back with the other engine."

Slocum waited a few minutes until he saw the grumbling men begin to work moving the supplies toward the other set of track going up into the mountains. He trailed after Melody and her father, still keeping a sharp eye out for any sign that Maguire had created dissension in the camp. He didn't find it. After the initial grumbling, the men had started singing as they worked, lugging the new hoard from Denver toward the other tracks. When they spied the kegs of whiskey the work went even faster.

Slocum never found the woman and her father. The engine from upslope came chugging back down and screeched to a halt. Maguire jumped off and began directing the men to load the new equipment. When the foreman saw Slocum, he yelled for Slocum to join him.

"How's it look at the end of the line?" Slocum asked.

"Better and worse than I thought," Maguire said. "With luck we might be able to get a two week jump on getting the track down. Bad part's the type of rock. Some looks like cheese, and well nigh as soft. Can't hold any track but it blasts quick."

Slocum shook his head. He had seen rock like that. It didn't blast well. There wasn't any way of telling how little—or how much—would come tumbling down.

"What are you going to do?" asked Slocum.

"What can we do? We push harder," Maguire said. "The other company's track is no good. Narrow gage and not worth the dynamite it'd take to blow it up. So we rip it up, enlarge the track bed, and put our own track down."

"Both rails?"

"What do you mean?" Maguire peered at Slocum curiously.

"Do you have to pull up both existing rails? What if you left one and only laid the other."

"I just said the track's no good. Those fools didn't know how to lay a proper rail."

Slocum wondered if this was another way Maguire might slow work. "If you needed to just add one track, wouldn't the work go faster?"

"Yes, of course, but—"

"You can come back in the spring and do it right."

"The track's not in good shape. Been up there an entire winter, and the bed's not quite level. They didn't take one whit of pride in their bloody work."

"But would it last the winter?" Slocum pressed.

"Might," Maguire said grudgingly. "Might speed up work if we needed to just check half the rail and add to the other. Ye got a good head on your shoulders, Slocum, ye do indeed. Hop on. We're goin' up to check this out."

Slocum swung onto the engine beside the foreman. Maguire leaned out and waved the workers back. They had loaded the train in record time, and Maguire wasn't going to let any time go to waste. The engine began chugging along, slowly at first, then with increasing speed and power. Slocum had never been up into Widowmaker Pass before. The ride was enough to make him long for a horse. Some parts of the route showed him a thousand foot drop to the side of the train. Other parts made him feel closed in and antsy, the rock walls rising up less than a foot on either side of the train, but when the engine burst free and the fireman began stoking furiously, Slocum knew they were on the final incline.

He chanced a look to the side and saw the sheer drop. It might not match earlier falls, but this was rugged and straight down. In the distance he saw a green river weaving its way through the canyon floor. A rock tossed over the side wouldn't hit for minutes, Slocum guessed.

"Quite a sight, ain't it, Slocum, me laddy buck?"

"It is that," Slocum said. He usually wasn't impressed by such things. This time he was. And equally as impressive as the natural beauty of the canyon and the mountains was the engineering it had taken getting the track laid this far. Ahead, Slocum saw why they called it Widowmaker Pass.

"Nasty bit of work, ain't it?" asked Maguire, shouting over the grinding of the engine and the slipping of steel wheels on the steep track. "That rock's got nowhere to go when it comes out. We have to load it on the train and move it back to a canyon where we dump it over."

"Can't you use some of it for the roadbed?"

"Damned little," admitted Maguire. "I got men workin' around the clock to get through here. It's that important, Slocum. We get through here and the rest is a cakewalk on into Cameron."

Slocum had to agree. He didn't know much about laying track, but he had worked a bit with explosives and knew how to blast hard rock. The pass was going to be hell.

"Jump on down. Here's our new base camp." Maguire swung off the engine and hit the ground running. Slocum followed a few seconds later, being sure to keep his feet under him. He had an instant's flight of fancy that he started running, couldn't stop, and ended up in midair, looking down a thousand feet.

"I'm keeping the men workin' round the clock. That's the only way to get through in time."

"Bergstrom had some idea there was going to be an early snow."

"Thought so," said Maguire. "I been checkin' out the woolly worms. Heavy coats. Means a big winter. And the squirrels? You've seen them now, haven't ye, Slocum? Bushy tails and they're puttin' away heaps of nuts. A sure sign of snow soon, and it's likely to last a long time once it falls."

Slocum shrugged this off. He had never seen real evidence that caterpillars or squirrels knew anything about the weather that a clever man couldn't figure out on his own, but he accepted Maguire's appraisal of the signs. Slocum had known more than one farmer who relied heavily on such evidence to know when to get in crops and when to plant in the spring after the worst of the winter was past.

"I got two of my best men up in the pass blastin'," said Maguire. "You want to go—" He never finished his sentence. A deep rumble echoed from higher in Widowmaker Pass, the force of it knocking both Slocum and Maguire off their feet. They tumbled down and the repeated shaking of the ground kept them from getting up soon.

"What'n the bloody hell was that?" roared Maguire. "What's happenin'? Tell me, damn your eyes!" He reached out and grabbed a dazed worker stumbling by from the direction of the explosion.

"Blast went off premature. Trapped 'em both. Tons of rock. God, it was horrible!"

Maguire muttered to himself and plowed through the disorganized men to get to the front of the track. Rock had fallen across track already laid by the earlier railroad company, but Maguire didn't care about that. He grabbed a shovel and began working.

"Don't ye stand there, men. Put your back into it. Men are trapped here!"

Slocum was the first to obey. Alongside Maguire, he worked to pry heavy rock free and roll it away from the track. He wasn't quite sure how Maguire knew where to look for the two men trapped by the rockfall, but Slocum decided it was better to try to free them than to just stand around and let them perish.

Slocum was a betting man, but he wouldn't take any odds that the two were still alive, not under this avalanche.

"They measured the fuse and lit it but something went wrong. Burned too fast or something," one of the huge Irish trackmen said. "Burned just like that, lickety-split and it was gone and it all blowed up. Faith, I never saw—"

Slocum knew what had happened. Inexperienced workers had put the wrong fuse on their charge. Instead of burning at an inch per minute, it burned at a foot per minute. They hadn't had time to get free, and hadn't known the fuse was racing toward the black powder they were using to blast.

He glanced over at Gus Maguire. The foreman's jaw was set. His grim eyes met Slocum's. He knew what had happened, also. He dug faster. And Slocum was glad he hadn't bet against finding anyone alive under the rockfall.

A feebly twitching hand reached for daylight. Maguire and three others worked even faster. Slocum saw that the man had fallen between the rails. Together with the steel rail, a cavity in the roadbed had given him enough protection to keep him from being crushed.

"Matt," the man gasped. "Where's Matt? He was right behind me. I dived for cover, but Matt—"

Twenty minutes later they found the man's friend, crushed beyond recognition. Slocum led the party to dig a grave and put the body in it since few of the man's friends could bring themselves to help with the grisly chore. Finished, Slocum returned to the base camp. Maguire had ordered tea brewed for his men. They hunched over the strong brew, not looking up.

Slocum expected Maguire to berate them for such carelessness. Instead, he was urging them to work harder, to pay more attention to what they did, and to finish the tracks.

"It's not for Mr. Bergstrom, though it means his very life. It's not for Miss Melody. It's not even for me. It's for the people on the far side of Widowmaker Pass. They're cut off from supplies most of the year. Think of them. Think of poor Matthew O'Leary giving his life to make this pipe dream a reality."

Slocum saw the words stirring the crew. They finished their tea and returned to clear off the tracks and continue. Gus Maguire sat by himself at the edge of the camp, a tin cup of the potent tea in his hand. Slocum had drunk coffee that would take the hide off a mule, but this Irish tea was even stronger.

"They went on back to work. Can ye believe it, Slocum?"

"You inspired them, gave them something bigger than their paychecks to work for."

"Paychecks? I never mentioned money. Wouldn't do no good with this rowdy bunch."

"I see that," Slocum said. "Did you know the man who was killed?"

"Not all that well. His friend is something else. He's a lucky young man to be alive." Maguire stared into the bottom of his cup as if he could read the tea leaves and scry the future.

"You act like it was your fault."

"It was. I'm pushin' them to get the track done. They didn't know anything of blastin', but I let 'em do it because there was no one else. I killed that boy just as sure as if I put a pistol to his head."

Slocum thought a while on this. He heard nothing but sincere grief in Maguire's words.

"What happened outside the saloon last night? When Wall offered you a hundred dollars to slow work?"

"What?" Gus Maguire shot to his feet. He lumbered over and glared at Slocum. "You heard what that whoreson offered me, and ye think I took him up on it?"

"No, not now," Slocum said.

"I laughed in his face. Then I spit in it," Maguire raged. "There's not enough money in Anthony Parsons's coffers to buy this Mick! I'll dance on his grave, I will! And you, I thought better of ye, Slocum."

"You're paying me to be suspicious. I apologize for what I was thinking."

"I'm pushin' them all too hard, but we got to be through the pass in three weeks 'fore the snow comes. And that damned trestle. How long's it to take Parsons to get it built? How long, how long?" Maguire went off, muttering to himself.

Slocum worked on a cup of tea, then dashed the remains into the fire. He had been wrong about Gus Maguire. Now it was time to show him he didn't harbor any apprehension about him or his loyalty to Clarence Bergstrom.

9

The next week vanished in a blur of constant fatigue for Slocum. When he wasn't helping up in the pass with blasting, he stayed in the main camp outside Central City to fight off the increasingly vicious vandalism. The third night after O'Leary was killed, Slocum found a keg of powder near the small tent used to store the whiskey. He yanked the fuse out seconds before it would have detonated the powder, taking all the whiskey with it.

Slocum had tried to imagine what a fiery rain of alcohol on the camp would have done. He had shivered and pushed it from his mind. Two nights after that incident, he found half the horses in the corral poisoned and dying. He immediately checked and found his own steed wasn't affected by the bad grain given as feed. He had accosted the young boy responsible for the animals and had found nothing to implicate him in the wanton killing. Slocum had spent the next twenty minutes putting dying horses out of their misery. Each bullet used he imagined going through Emmett Wall's vile heart.

"They'll do the same to people," Clarence Bergstrom declared. "A horse, a man, it just doesn't matter to Parsons. He'll murder us all in our sleep."

Maguire coughed loudly and looked toward Slocum, silently urging him to put Bergstrom's fears to rest. It wasn't in Slocum to outright lie. He couldn't spend the entire night on patrol and hope to cover both the main camp and the new base camp up in Widowmaker Pass.

"I'll need more men if you want to keep this place bottled up tight," Slocum said. "I'm trying to cover the weakest points, the places where they can hit us the hardest."

"Such as?" Bergstrom was in no mood to argue with the hired hands. He wanted results and didn't think Slocum was giving them.

"How'd you like to have all your track dumped into the canyon?" Slocum asked. "Or maybe they'd do something nastier. A few extra charges set up in the rock in the middle of the pass would kill half the crew there."

"What are you doing to prevent this?"

"Dammit, I'm trying, but it's not possible for one man to be everywhere." Slocum was at the verge of telling the railroad baron to take his job. Slocum faced Emmett Wall and a dozen hired gunmen. There wasn't any way he could face up to them, not straight on. He had to fight a defensive war, and it rankled him as much as it did the foreman and the railroad's owner.

"Mr. Bergstrom, don't go too hard on him," Maguire cut in. "He's been doin' the work of three men. Helpin' out with the blastin' is just part of it. Slocum keeps a watch all night long."

"If he wouldn't keep so close a watch on my daughter, he'd have time to keep our livestock from being slaughtered," snapped Bergstrom.

"That was what I was hired to do," Slocum said coldly. "Your foreman worried about Miss Bergstrom's safety." He started to tell the man about Wall kidnapping his daughter, then stopped. Melody hadn't wanted her father to find out and had made him promise not to mention it. Slocum never broke his word unless there was a damned good reason. Being spiteful because he was dog-tired didn't even come close to giving him real justification.

"We've got other problems. I'm going to send Melody back to Denver and get her out of danger," Bergstrom said. "Will that let you put up a decent patrol of my property?"

Slocum knew the man was worrying about getting through Widowmaker Pass before the snow. The weather had turned measurably colder in the past few days, and reports kept trickling back that Anthony Parsons was almost finished with the trestle across Grand Gorge. It would be only a few days after the bridge was done before he could get a dozen miles of easy track laid and claim the government's reward. Clarence Bergstrom was in a race and was losing it.

"Do what you want," Slocum said. He wasn't going to argue. And Maguire saw that Slocum would pull up stakes and move on if Melody Bergstrom left the camp.

"Mr. Bergstrom, you're bein' a mite too harsh on Slocum. He's doin' us a good job."

"And more than that, Papa, I am not going to return to Denver. You told me to never quit once I started on something important." Melody Bergstrom came into the tent, her face flushed and her usually soft brown eyes blazing with anger. "I can be of help here and I will not be scared off."

"Melody, this doesn't concern you," Bergstrom said.

"It most certainly does. I have worked as hard as any man in this camp. I may not lay track or blast rock cliffs or use a six-shooter, but cooking and doctoring are difficult enough chores under any circumstances. With Parsons threatening us all, it isn't a good idea to send me back to Denver as if I were some mewling infant."

"You'll be safer, and you won't need Slocum's constant guard." Clarence Bergstrom looked fatigued and more than a little irked that his underlings, including his daughter, were arguing with him.

"That's why he was hired," Gus Maguire repeated, "to watch after Miss Melody."

Slocum saw the change in Bergstrom. He had greeted Slocum's watchfulness originally. Slocum wondered what had changed. He had dozens of wanted posters on him drifting throughout the West. He didn't think Bergstrom had seen one, but someone might have said something in Central City. Bergstrom had been there several times talking with Sheriff Lake. The sheriff might have found a poster.

Slocum pushed that notion out of his head. The sheriff was a decent man, a law-abiding one. If he had seen a wanted poster—or if it had been brought to his attention by Emmett Wall—he would have arrested Slocum and not given it a second thought.

"We need to concentrate on getting over the pass. I'm sorry, Melody. You have to return to Denver. There'll be a train going back tomorrow noon."

"No."

Bergstrom's eyes widened. He turned to his daughter and asked, "Are you defying me?"

"I most certainly am!"

Slocum had seen the fire in the woman before. That was part of what attracted him so to her. She was smart and quick and lovely and she had the spirit that made for a real woman. Standing up to her father like this wasn't a battle Slocum wanted to see, but it only fixed Melody's qualities even more firmly in his heart and mind.

Clarence Bergstrom seemed to collapse. For a moment Slocum thought he was going to break down and cry.

"What am I doing to myself?" Bergstrom moaned. "I'm ruining my family. Is any railroad worth it?"

"This one is, Papa." Melody went and knelt at his knee. She took his hand in hers and pressed her cheek against it. Maguire motioned for Slocum to leave.

The foreman and Slocum edged from the tent, leaving father and daughter to work out their problems. Slocum knew how this was going to end. The Denver and Utah Railroad might not win the government contract and reward, but Melody Bergstrom wasn't going to be sent back to Denver like a wayward schoolgirl.

"He don't mean a thing by this, Slocum. Ye can see how distraught the man is," Maguire said when they were away from the tent. "He sees us fallin' behind Parsons and his crew and lets it gnaw at his gut."

"There's no way I can keep Wall's hired guns from destroying us one bit at a time," Slocum said. "I can't patrol all night and work all day."

"We're tryin' to get a powder monkey in from Denver. He might be arrivin' come that noon train from Denver." Maguire let out a long, pent-up breath. It turned to silver feathers in the cold mountain air. "Ye sleep in the day and keep watch at night. I'll see that Mr. Bergstrom don't go botherin' ye none."

"I didn't want Melody getting into a row with him," Slocum said.

"She can take good care of herself. That colleen's a strong-willed lady." Maguire winked broadly as he added, "But then, that's nothin' you ain't already found for yourself, now is it, Slocum?"

Slocum shook his head ruefully. The foreman was right. The worst thing about the long night patrols wasn't the fear of getting cut down by Emmett Wall's gunmen, it was thinking about Melody Bergstrom. Long nights meant he had no time to spend with her.

"I'll keep the vermin from the camp, at least one more night," he said.

"That's all anyone can ask. Now don't go gettin' your nose out of joint over this, either. I'll see if Mr. Bergstrom might be able to offer ye more for the job."

"Forget that," Slocum said. "Hiring someone who could watch my back would suit me more."

"I'll see to it."

Slocum started on his rounds. He had several high points where he could sit down, not be outlined against the nighttime sky, and watch portions of the camp. Even so, getting in and out was ridiculously easy, because he couldn't be everywhere at once. Poisoning the horses had been the single most diabolical crime, in Slocum's eyes. The animals were innocent of anything their masters might do. If Wall and Parsons had a quarrel, it was with the men who rode the horses, not the beasts themselves.

Checking the supply tents revealed the usual number of workmen trying to get more than their share of the whiskey. Slocum chased them off, knowing that Bergstrom didn't want them making any more trips into Central City. The base camp had almost served it purpose, but Bergstrom wisely, in Slocum's opinion, kept a presence here to act as rear guard if Anthony Parsons tried anything more than petty vandalism.

Poking his nose in a few other tents, Slocum found a poker game in progress, two men passed out drunk, and more than a few snoring heavily after their labors. He stopped and stared at the tent with a single lamp inside. He saw Melody's outline against the canvas and watched for several minutes, tormenting himself with her nearness. He didn't dare stop and see if she was all right. He knew she was. Any time spent with her was time taken away from protecting the camp.

Slocum damned his bad luck in this respect. He ought to be able to take a few minutes off to be with the lovely woman. Instead, he stood and stared at her silhouette against a canvas curtain, separated by more than distance. He swung his rifle over his shoulder, military marching fashion, and went to find the first of his sentry posts. He could see both her tent and the supplies from this rise. Later he would work around and be sure that no sabotage was done to the track already laid.

He shivered at the thought of a few spikes being pulled out farther up the canyon. The steep drops meant a train hitting a loose rail would slip to one side, find no support on the roadbed, and then continue down a long drop to the river below. Men would die and the Denver and Utah would be bankrupt. He saw no way Clarence Bergstrom could ever recover from such a loss of men and machines.

Fighting a defensive war wasn't the way to win, Slocum decided as he crouched down in a tiny hollow protecting him from the wind. They had to take the fight straight to Parsons. Thoughts of the rickety trestle kept returning. The Rocky Mountain Rail Line didn't intend to run a regular schedule over that bridge. A few well-placed charges would knock the supports from under it. Slocum imagined the sight of the timbers falling majestically into the same river he had earlier imagined holding the Denver and Utah steam engine.

Reflexes faster than a cat's, Slocum swung around, rifle leveled, when he heard the grate of stone against stone. He squinted to close his eyes and adapt them even more to the darkness. He strained and heard someone moving back down the slope. Maguire had warned his workers about leaving camp for any reason. Slocum wasn't worried about shooting one of the Irishmen by accident.

He slithered up to the top of the rock that had been protecting him from the sharp wind blowing off the Rockies. He saw an indistinct shadow moving away, and another joined it. Slocum heaved a deep sigh. It was time for him to earn his money. Emmett Wall had sent his henchmen back to bedevil them.

Slocum pulled back the hammer on his Winchester and aimed carefully for the center of the largest shadow. He pulled the trigger and all hell broke loose.

The instant they spotted his muzzle flash, a half dozen gunmen opened fire. They had laid a trap for him and he had fallen into it. Bullets flying everywhere, Slocum scampered back across the boulder for cover.

The dull click of a six-shooter hammer coming back alerted him an instant before he heard Emmett Wall say in a cold voice, "Rot in hell, Slocum."

The bullet spun Slocum around and sent him rolling down the slope toward the Denver and Utah camp.

10

Slocum rolled and rolled and rolled, the razor-edged rocks slicing at his face and body, until he thought he would die of a thousand cuts. He finally came to rest at the bottom of the slope, just barely conscious after the long fall. He was aware of bullets tearing into the rocky soil around him, but he couldn't move, no matter how hard he tried. His legs were paralyzed and every breath caused a wracking shudder to pass through him. That cracked rib he had ridden into Central City with hadn't healed fully. He wanted to return fire, to get even with Wall for dry-gulching him like that.

His body refused to respond, and this saved his life.

In the distance, he heard Emmett Wall say, "He's had it, boys. Get after the track. Rip 'em up good. I don't want a section left between here and Widowmaker Pass."

Slocum tried again to force his way to his hands and knees. He had to protect the track already laid by the Denver and Utah workers. Wall would destroy weeks of work in a few minutes. Slocum tried to stand and simply exhausted himself. He lay facedown in the dirt, trying to catch his breath.

He heard boot steps approaching. He struggled to reach his six-shooter still resting in its cross-draw holster. His arms had turned to lead and refused to obey.

"I thought you were smarter'n this, Slocum. You're one stupid son of a bitch."

"Yeah, Emmett," another voice said. "And he's dead, too!"

The men laughed at this. Slocum heard them walking away. He tried once more to get to his ebony-handled Colt. Two quick shots would take out both bushwhackers. He tried and again he failed. Slocum stopped trying and collapsed, passing out.

When he came to, a pungent odor filled his nostrils. Slocum heaved and brought himself up to hands and knees. Another effort got him to his feet. He knew the smell and he knew what it meant. Staggering, barely keeping his feet, he turned toward the Denver and Utah track. Using his nose as a guide, he homed in on the dynamite Wall had planted.

Slocum fell facedown as he reached for the fuse on the six sticks of dynamite. His fingers tried closing and failed. He fought a rising tide of darkness welling inside. He couldn't pass out again. If he did, the track would be blown to hell and gone and so would he.

Slocum exerted supreme effort to grab the dynamite and throw it far away. He reached and he blacked out again.

He was jerked back to consciousness by a sharp burning in his left hand. He focused his eyes and saw that his hand had fallen across the black miner's fuse and had snuffed it out. Slocum didn't yank his hand back. He might be wrong. He inched forward until he could see what was happening more clearly. His hand had put out the fuse. He carefully pulled the fuse and the detonator cap from the middle of the dynamite. He tossed the cap as hard as he could.

It clattered a few feet away and went off with a bright flash and a loud pop. Slocum sat and stared at the dynamite in his hand. He had been damned lucky not to have been blown up with the track. Then he started thinking more rationally. He had found one charge. Wall wasn't the kind to rely on a single blast to wreck everything.

Slocum, on hands and knees, began working his way down the track. He found two more bombs. The first hadn't been set properly and the fuse had come loose from the detonator cap; it was harmless. The second he reached seconds before it was to go off. He had regained enough strength to grab the four sticks taped together and heave with all his might. This time he reached the canyon edge. He saw the dynamite rebound from the verge, then slip over the side. Less than a second later a loud explosion rocked the area, its echo magnified and rolling down Grand Gorge.

Slocum sat and tried to get back his strength. He had to keep going. There might be more. He had come in just one direction. There would be other charges, up toward Widowmaker Pass.

"What in the Sam Hill's happened to ye, Slocum?"

Slocum didn't recognize the voice. He grabbed for his Colt, only to find the leather thong was still in place over the hammer. He tried to get his weapon free and couldn't do it.

"John, stop!"

He looked up and saw the dim figures closing in around him. He thought he heard Melody Bergstrom's voice telling him not to draw.

"Melody?"

"John, what's happened to you? You're a sight!" Arms circled him and held him close. He tried to get away, to protect the railroad. He found he couldn't get away.

"Is he gonna use that six-shooter of his?" Gus Maguire asked.

"No, he's just shaken up," Melody said.

Slocum felt as if his brain floated above his body and watched, totally divorced from all normal sensation. He wondered if this was what it was like being a ghost.

"Dynamite," he croaked. "Wall planted dynamite all along the track. Stopped three. Couldn't—ambushed me. No way."

He sagged back into Melody's arms.

He heard Maguire shouting orders to check the length of track. In the distance, another explosion went off, and then another and another. Slocum had no idea if they came together or were separated by long hours. He drifted in and out of consciousness. When he came back to his full senses, he was inside a lamp-lit tent. What he noticed first was the subtle odor in the tent.

"Perfume?" he asked, looking around. Melody sat on a small stool before a folding desk. She looked up and smiled.

"You say the strangest things, John. I suppose that is what you're smelling. I get it from Denver."

"It's nice." He forced himself to a full sitting position against her wishes. "I'll be fine. Did Maguire save the track?"

"Only one charge went off and did any significant damage. The men threw the dynamite into the canyon before it destroyed much else. Wall avoided the camp and went for the track, the son of a bitch!"

Such language from the genteel woman startled Slocum. Then he realized Melody was as involved in getting the government award as her father. Feelings had to run high when your competitor tried such underhanded tactics to win.

"Parsons didn't have any call doing this," she said. "He'll probably win fair and square, but he had to be sure. Never take a chance, that's Anthony Parsons."

"How much damage was done?" he asked.

"Gus said it'll take a week or longer to repair it adequately to keep freight moving up into the pass. There's one good thing. The engine is on the pass side of the damage. We can hand-carry the rails, food, and equipment across the ripped-up section to the train and keep the upper camp supplied."

"That'll be quite a chore," Slocum said.

"We have no other choice. John, thank you for stopping them."

"I didn't do that good a job." He looked at his tattered clothing. Rolling down the hill had ripped him up something fierce. He felt the blood oozing down a dozen places Melody hadn't patched. Stretching caused lances of pain to jab down into his body, but Slocum kept at it. In a few minutes, the agony receded and was bearable. He could move, walk—and fight back.

"Where do you think you're going?" she asked when she saw that he intended to leave. "You can sleep here tonight. No one's going to gossip, if that's what you're afraid of."

"I don't rightly care about that on my part," Slocum said, "And you're able to take care of your own reputation."

Melody Bergstrom grinned almost savagely. "I don't mind it at all when you're taking care of it for me."

"I've got work to do."

"John," she said in exasperation. "You're in no condition to go back out there to look for more dynamite. Gus has his men on the line. They're better able to deal with this." She stared at him and slowly realized he had no intention of walking the tracks hunting for more bombs.

"John, no!" she cried.

He was out of the tent and into the darkness, hiding from her, before she could get to her feet. Melody stood in the tent and peered into the night, crying out for him to come back. Slocum waited in the shadows until she gave up and went back into her tent. Only then did he move toward his own tent. He had to get spare cylinders for his Colt Navy if he was going to be in any kind of a gunfight. Reloading was simpler and faster simply dropping already loaded cylinders into the percussion cap six-shooter.

Melody must have alerted the foreman, because Maguire and several men came looking for Slocum, but he eluded them. He knew what he had to do, and it wasn't anything for them to get mixed up in. Slocum felt as if he had been pulled backward through a knothole and had missed dying by a stroke of luck. Emmett Wall would have filled him with lead if he hadn't thought Slocum was already dead.

Slocum stretched and felt the plaster patch on his shoulder where Melody had fixed him up. Wall's bullet hadn't done much damage, but he had fired at such close range that the impact had spun Slocum around and sent him rolling down the hill. Slocum practiced his draw a few times; the bullet hole in his left shoulder didn't bother him. He was ready for the fight.

He got to the corral, saddled, and mounted before Maguire could stop him. He rode into the darkness with the foreman shouting after him. Slocum kept riding fast until he got halfway to Central City. He reined in and considered the fire glowing in his gut. Revenge pure and simple drove him. He didn't cotton much to Wall or Parsons or what they had done to stop the Denver and Utah Railroad from laying their tracks, but that wasn't enough to maybe get himself killed over.

Slocum had to admit even Melody Bergstrom wasn't enough for that. He had rescued her because he had been able to, but riding into the teeth of the Rocky Mountain Rail Line guns wasn't something he'd do for anyone.

But he would ride into the enemy camp for revenge. He had a powerful score to settle with Emmett Wall and only the foreman's death would satisfy Slocum.

As he neared the camp, he thought about the best way of getting back at Wall. Putting a bullet through his putrid heart would be best, but Slocum wanted the man to squirm a mite first. Let him know he wasn't invincible behind his barricade of hired gunmen. Let him taste the bitterness of fear before he died. Then Slocum would finish him off quick-like, even if the man deserved a slow death.

Slocum reined back and looked at the way the camp was spread out. The number of patrols didn't matter to him; he was going in even if he faced an entire army, but he didn't think the odds would be all that bad tonight. He heard sounds of celebration drifting up. Some of the men might be in Central City saloons boozing it up. Others were here, also congratulating themselves on how badly they had damaged Bergstrom's railroad.

They wouldn't expect to see a man they thought was dead riding into their camp. To them Slocum was a ghost. And this ghost was going to even the score.

The trestle was a dark patch on an even darker canyon. At the bottom of Grand Gorge roared the river that would soon carry the bridge downstream. Slocum had seen the slipshod way the trestle was constructed. It wouldn't be hard to bring down the entire structure.

He dismounted less than a mile outside the camp and went the rest of the way on foot. Every step he took erased that much more of the stiffness from the long fall down the side of the hill. By the time he saw the first sentry, he was ready to wrestle grizzlies and hogtie them with rattlesnakes.

The sentry walked past him, not even knowing Slocum was behind. Slocum drew his Colt Navy and swung it in an arc that ended at the back of the man's head. The sentry fell face forward and lay unmoving. Slocum stuffed the man's six-shooter into his own belt and then took his rifle. Never leave firearms behind when they might be useful—or used against you. Slocum kept on walking in the direction the sentry was patrolling. He took out two more men and found himself laden with six-shooters and rifles. He emptied the rifles' magazines and smashed the barrels against rocks until they wouldn't shoot without blowing up. Then he boldly walked straight into the camp.

Men sang and shouted and drank whiskey, but these weren't the workers. The Celestials were already asleep in their section of the camp. Slocum saw them as innocent victims. It would be too easy to go into their area and shoot them up, killing enough to frighten the others. But he had only pity for them. They were hardly more than slaves to Anthony Parsons.

He walked less than ten feet away from three men he recognized as being Wall's henchmen. Of the foreman he saw nothing. That didn't matter. Revenge was going to be sweet.

Slocum went to the tracks that ran into the distance and ended somewhere outside Denver. But his interest stopped at a siding.

The tracks parted at a switch and formed a siding where several flatcars laden with heavy steel track were stored. Slocum checked the switch and saw that Wall hadn't bothered putting a padlock on it. Anybody could throw it and shift from the main track to the siding—and when Slocum did, the heavy flatcars would start rolling out onto the almost-finished trestle.

"How much weight can that bridge hold?" he asked himself, smiling grimly. The answer was apparent. Three flatcars weighed down with steel rails and drilling equipment would collapse the trestle. And even if it didn't collapse, the track ended abruptly near where the middle of the bridge would be. The flatcars would simply roll off the track and into the deep gorge. Parsons could afford to lose the equipment, but he'd have to replace it. That would delay him a week or longer, Slocum guessed.

Even this small sabotage wasn't adequate payback for the damage done to the Denver and Utah tracks earlier.

No one paid him the least bit of attention as he threw the switch on the siding so that the flatcar would roll down the tracks and across the trestle. Slocum grunted and put his back into it to make sure the switch was locked in the position he wanted. Then he went to the leading flatcar and looked it over. A hand brake had been set. He spun the locking wheel several times and released the brake and waited.

Nothing happened.

Slocum jumped to the ground and checked the wheels. Wall was taking no chances. He had put wooden wedges under all four steel wheels. Slocum kicked them out. When the last one was knocked free, he thought there was something more holding the flatcar in place. He watched and waited and it seemed to just sit.

Then he noticed a small movement. The heavily laden car took time to get moving. Slocum stepped out of the way as

the flatcar gathered speed. Before it reached the switch that
would send it across the trestle, Slocum was working on the
second flatcar.

The loud rumble of wheels clattering against steel tracks
alerted Wall and the others in Parsons's camp that something was seriously wrong. They shouted and ran out to
stop the flatcar. They might as well have tried to stop an
avalanche by waving their hats. The ponderously heavy car
rattled past them.

"Get up there and set the brake, damn your eyes!" bellowed Wall.

Slocum saw one brave man try. Slocum released the hand
brake on the second flatcar and got it started on its way, and
this time it had a passenger. He rode on top of the stack of
steel rails, the two captured rifles at his side. He drew two
of the captured six-shooters and began firing wildly at the
other car. He wasn't certain that he hit the man trying to
stop the other car, but the effect was the same. The man
fell off and hit the ground hard.

The flatcar kept rolling.

"It'll break the barricade protecting the bridge. Stop it,
stop the damned thing!" Emmett Wall was beside himself, and there wasn't anything he could do. He had to
stand and watch the juggernaut race down the track, across
the wobbly trestle, and smash into the barricade at the
end.

Slocum cursed his bad luck. The barricade held. But he
had loosed the second car. The first had battered the wood
restraints at the end of the track to the breaking point. The
second car would be all it took to destroy the bridge and
cost Anthony Parsons a healthy sum for replacement of rails
and equipment.

"It's him! Goddamn, it's Slocum!" someone cried as
Slocum rode past on the second flatcar.

Slocum opened up with the six-shooters and drove the
men to cover. When both hammers fell on empty cylinders,
he tossed the guns aside and began firing with two more

captured pistols. These emptied, he began working with the rifles.

A few bullets came his way, but not enough to deter him. He kept the men from getting aboard and applying the hand brake. When the flatcar hit the flimsy track at the end of the bridge, Slocum jumped off and hit the ground hard, rolling to absorb the impact.

He lost the second rifle in the fall, but he didn't care. He still had his trusty six-gun and three replacement cylinders for it, enough firepower to get him out of any tight spot. Slocum came to his knees and watched the flatcar rolling over the bridge. Timbers screeched as they strained to hold up the additional weight bearing down on them. The entire bridge began shaking as the track began giving way.

"No, stop it, stop it!" he heard Wall wailing.

Slocum laughed when the second flatcar rammed into the first and shoved it through the barricade. Both cars rolled off the end. A savage tearing sound ripped through the air as the end of the trestle came apart, nails pulling free, timbers breaking, track twisting loose.

Long seconds later, the sound of the flatcars striking the bottom of Grand Gorge echoed up to him. He hadn't destroyed the trestle, but he had definitely slowed Parsons for a week or longer.

Slocum got to his feet and slipped through deep shadows to get away from the camp. A few shots sang through the air, seeking his flesh. None came close enough to make him take cover. The confusion he had created prevented Wall from mounting a concerted effort to find him. Those hunting for him searched aimlessly.

Slocum found his horse and rode slowly back to the Denver and Utah camp, some measure of revenge already his. He had paid Parsons back for his sabotage. All that remained was evening the score with Emmett Wall. And he would.

11

Slocum rode back into the Denver and Utah camp feeling good, in spite of the pains starting to take their toll on his body. Emmett Wall and his henchmen had waltzed into camp when Slocum was guarding it and had done their worst. He had returned the favor.

And Slocum thought he'd done a better job of it. The trestle was rickety and would topple if they didn't take care going out to repair it. The sight of the flatcars loaded with steel rails and drilling equipment toppling into Grand Gorge made him warm inside.

He had taken the fight to them and had won. It would be a while before Anthony Parsons tried to get even, Slocum thought. He had been shown that Clarence Bergstrom wasn't a toothless lion, that he could fight back—would.

"John!" came the immediate call from the direction of the camp. "Where did you go? I was so worried!"

He saw Melody Bergstrom running toward him. He dismounted and walked the rest of the way to her. She threw her arms around his neck and almost smothered him. He decided this was about the best medicine for what ailed him.

"Been on a little errand," he said simply.

"I thought you were going to get yourself killed. Gus said you were going to try to gun down Wall."

"Wouldn't do anything that stupid, not feeling like I do."

"But where did you go?" She stared at him. A look of horror slowly spread. "You *did* try to kill him. What happened? Did you—"

"Wall's still just fine, leastwise as far as I could determine," Slocum said. He wondered what Parsons might do to his foreman after tonight. Parsons had to be paying those hired guns plenty to keep such unpleasantness from happening, and they had all failed miserably. If Parsons found out only one man had done all that damage to his railroad, he would be fit to be tied. Slocum hoped he didn't take out too much of his ire on Wall. Slocum wanted the foreman for himself. And Wall had only begun to suffer.

"You went into their camp. What did you do?"

"You'll be hearing about it tomorrow, I reckon," Slocum said. He stretched and groaned slightly. His minor injuries were coming back to haunt him. He had been kept moving through the need for revenge and sheer determination. Now that he was free of Parsons's camp, his body was telling him it was time to rest. Slocum didn't quite fall into Melody's arms, but he found himself being supported by the woman.

"Now will you listen to reason, John?" she asked sternly.

"Show me the way to your bed," he said. And she did.

"I can't condone such goings on," Clarence Bergstrom said, but the smile on his lips told a story different from his words. "We've here to build railroads, not destroy them."

"How much damage did ye say was done to Parsons's fine trestle?" asked Gus Maguire, obviously gloating. He looked from his boss to Slocum and back, knowing full well the source of Anthony Parsons's catastrophe.

"He lost well nigh a thousand dollars worth of rolling stock and supplies, mostly steel rail, but the real damage came to his trestle. He was fuming mad and said it'd take him more'n two weeks to repair it."

"He's lying," Slocum said. "He'll have it fixed in a week, maybe less. There wasn't that much damage done to it."

Under his breath Maguire said, "Dammit."

"We don't know anything about this matter," Bergstrom said. "I've informed Sheriff Lake of that. Now, let's put this unpleasant subject behind us and get on to another."

"*Our* supplies," whispered Melody, sitting close to Slocum. He wondered how her father liked the idea of her personally nursing him back to health. He hadn't been able to do much during the night, but the feel of her soft body rubbing against him had been better medicine than anything else she had done.

"We need to get into Denver and restock. The additional rail we used to repair the parts destroyed by the explosions has taken away from our meager inventory. Then there are other items our men require." Bergstrom cleared his throat and looked hard at Maguire. "Please try to keep the consumption of whiskey to a minimum. I know the men were celebrating this morning, but—"

"I'll do what I can, Mr. Bergstrom," Maguire said. "If you're goin' into Denver, could I send a list of wares I'll be needin' when we get through the pass?"

"Very well. I intend to leave when the train arrives at noon, and my daughter and Mr. Slocum will be accompanying me." Bergstrom looked at Slocum. "I think it is best that you see a doctor for your injuries. From all my daughter has said, they might be more serious than they appear."

"Sir, I'm just a mite scratched up." Slocum stirred slightly, aware of the tightness in his left shoulder where Wall had plugged him. He looked at Melody, who shook her head slightly, cautioning him to silence.

"I can see blood on your shirt, sir. Fresh blood, from the look of it. You'll go with us. That matter is closed. Melody,

get what you'll need for the trip. Slocum, do likewise, and
be back here by noon." Bergstrom turned to his foreman
and began discussing what they needed and what they could
afford.

Slocum and Melody left, and he didn't mind having her
support him more than he needed.

"This surely is one fancy car," Slocum said, looking up
and down the length of the sleeper coach. Gilt decorated
the metal parts and a large bed dominated the side of the
room, providing hardly enough space to get by. A table
with a simple meal had been set out at the far end. Slocum
decided he could get used to living like this, if he had to.
But that wasn't going to happen any time soon.

"You ought to see Papa's," said Melody. "He bought his
from General Palmer, and the general always travels first-
class, no matter where he goes. I do declare, he probably
has a small house pulled along when he goes riding."

Slocum eyed the fixtures and saw what it meant to be
rich. Clarence Bergstrom didn't flaunt his wealth; Slocum
knew the man was putting everything into getting the Denver and Utah track across Widowmaker Pass to win the
government contract, but if this was what the man had
to fall back on, the rich were very different from common folks.

"Where do I bunk?" Slocum asked. He stretched and felt
the healing wound tighten on him. Riding in a freight car
or in a mail car, if there was one, would be a chore, but
nothing he couldn't bear up to.

"Why, you're riding with me, right here, John. Unless
that doesn't suit you." She was toying with him. Melody
batted her lashes in his direction and gave him that wicked
smile that was anything but a little girl's. "I supposed you
could ride up in the engine with the fireman and engineer,
if you prefer."

Slocum considered the offer. He didn't know how much
freedom Clarence Bergstrom gave his daughter. The last

thing he wanted was for the railroad magnate to come swinging through and find his precious daughter in the arms of the hired help. Slocum knew he'd be lucky to end up dangling from a mail hook in some jerkwater station if that happened.

"Why are you hesitating? Don't you find me attractive?" She came to him and held him close, then tipped her face upward for him to kiss. Her eyes were closed and she was waiting. Slocum knew it wouldn't do to deny her. Hell had no fury like a woman scorned, and he had no intention of doing that to Melody Bergstrom.

But her father—

"John," she said sharply. "What is wrong?"

"What if your father—"

"Oh, silly, don't you think I value my privacy? I have the doors locked. We're the last coach, and there's no traffic through here. We have the car all to ourselves."

Slocum looked at the well-appointed car once more and decided he could get used to this kind of luxury real fast. He kissed Melody, and then she returned the kiss with enough fervor to take his breath away. He felt himself getting wobbly in the knees and staggered. Together they fell to the bed.

"Whoa, wait," he said. "I'm feeling a bit shaky."

"It's not you, silly," Melody said. "The train's pulled out of the camp. We're on our way to Denver."

Slocum knew the train would average less than twenty miles an hour through the mountains and a bit better than that once it hit the far side and got to steaming on into Denver. That gave them at least ten hours to enjoy the gentle rocking of the train.

"Your pa won't come busting in?"

"Hardly." Her fingers worked at his gun belt and got it free. Melody dropped it on the floor and started working on his boots. "You really should rest. In bed. With me!"

The next few minutes were anything but a rest for Slocum. He had his hands full of a writhing, moving, kissing, teasing, lively young woman. The rocking of the train added to his disorientation and, by the time he had regained his balance, he was buck naked on the bed, and so was Melody.

She sat up on her knees, looking down at his groin. Her fingers reached out and touched his growing manhood. He groaned softly as she gripped down harder, stroking, tugging, gently massaging until he was stiffer than a steel spike.

For his part Slocum enjoyed the sight before him. Melody's large breasts swayed gently with the motion of the train. Every curve in the course caused her breasts to jiggle just a bit more, the coppery tips growing even as he watched. Slocum reached out and cupped those succulent melons and squeezed down just as she was doing on him. The woman threw her head back, closed her eyes and let out a long, low sigh of delight.

"That's so nice, John. So nice! Keep doing it!"

One hand remained on the fleshy mounds, moving from the left to the right and then back, teasing the nubbin at each summit before moving on. The other hand stroked along her sleek side, found a fleshy thigh, and moved inward.

His hand brushed over the dark, fleecy patch nestled between her legs. She was already damp with need for him. His fingers explored a little, stroking slickly up and down along her nether lips. Melody shivered like a falling leaf in a high wind, then sank forward onto his muscular form.

"Now, John, do it now. Hurry."

"We've got hours," he protested. He wanted to make this last. He grunted when she squeezed down emphatically on his hard length.

"Now!" she cried. "We can do it again later, but I need you now. I need *this* now." She tugged at him to let him know exactly what she desired most from him.

The pressure mounting in Slocum's loins reached the point where he didn't think he could control himself. He let the rocking motion of the train carry him over so he was on top. The brunette quickly spread her thighs in wanton invitation. He moved into position, the soft bed taking some of the shock as the train hit a rough section of track.

"Get in, John, hurry. I want you inside when we get to the next section. It's even rougher than this was."

Slocum moved his hips forward, sinking slowly into the woman's demanding depths. When he was completely surrounded by her clinging, moist flesh, he paused to revel in the carnal heat. He felt his balls tensing, preparing to jettison their milky load. He held back. There would be more, better.

And there was.

The train hit the rough section of track Melody had desired. The motion of the train caused Slocum to move back and forth with little effort. He let the train throw him from side to side, his long stalk stirring inside the woman. Melody moaned and began thrashing around. The motion of the train was just about perfect. In, out, back, forth, the pitching action carried him deeper and deeper into her.

"Yes, oh, yes, this is it, what I wanted, oh, yes, oh!"

Slocum began moving, adding his motion to that of the train. He grew tighter in the balls, his belly muscles tensing as he rammed forward repeatedly. Melody's fingers laced through his lank black hair, pulling him down. His lips closed on her nipples, moving back and forth until the hard little nubbins throbbed. He pressed his tongue into the left nipple and felt her distant heart beating wildly.

Her fingers moved from his hair to his neck, across his shoulders, and finally back and forth across his back. He winced slightly as her fingernails dug into his already tortured flesh, but he wasn't going to protest. He was lost completely in a carnal paradise, the train adding to his every motion.

"More, more," she muttered to herself. "So fine, so fine!"

He moved more rapidly, unable to hold back. A new patch of rough track made Melody's body rise and fall around him, stimulating new and different areas. Her fingers raked his back and he finally lost all control. As he did, he heard her cry out in desire.

They sank down to the soft bed, locked in one another's arms. Slocum moved to kiss her as she snuggled even closer, her legs wrapped around his in a Gordian knot.

"That was just what I needed, John. I hope you're not too tired."

"I'm a mite spent," he allowed.

"Then we'll have to entice you, won't we?" she said, her fingers lightly stroking his flaccid organ. "There are three more sections of track between here and Denver I simply will *not* miss."

And they didn't.

12

The train pulled into Denver just a little before dawn after two minor breakdowns that left Clarence Bergstrom huffing and puffing worse than the steam engine.

"Papa, don't let it worry you. There wasn't any sign of sabotage by Parsons. These things *do* break down now and again," Melody said, trying to soothe her father. Slocum saw that the man wasn't likely to be mollified, and Melody didn't succeed.

"Dammit, why now?" the man raged. "This is important. I need to get those supplies moving. Time's a-wastin'!"

"You probably couldn't have gotten it loaded before dawn, anyway," Slocum said. "Most stores don't stay open around the clock." In spite of his good sense, this didn't keep Bergstrom from pacing back and forth, ranting more and causing the men around him to look nervously for an escape route.

Slocum didn't mind the delay. It had given him a chance to jump into his clothes, go help with the minor problems, then return to Melody. He wasn't sure which he considered the rest and which he considered the most tiring. The woman was insatiable in bed, as if she had a lifetime of passion locked up and waiting to release only when he climbed in bed with her. Slocum wasn't going to complain, but he was beginning to wonder where this might be leading.

He didn't think Melody Bergstrom considered him anything more than a pleasant companion to while away the tedious hours on the train, but he wasn't sure. The way she kept eyeing him made him uneasy. This was pure trouble, and he couldn't stop her. The mood her father was in meant any discretion on Slocum's part would cause a real blowup, one he wasn't able to do much about.

"Get the agent out on the platform. Have him waiting for us, by damn," Bergstrom called out.

"Sir, I can't use the telegraph while the train's highballin' along. We got to stop so I can climb a pole and hook the wires onto the telegraph line," Slocum said.

"Best to keep moving," Slocum said. "There's no need to send a telegram when we can be there in less than a half hour. Chances are good your agent's going to be ready for you. Wasn't he expecting us at midnight?"

"He was," grumbled Bergstrom. The man prowled his car looking for things to criticize.

"Papa, calm down. This isn't doing any of us good." Melody laid her hand on her father's shoulder. The man never stopped his restless pacing. Slocum had seen caged animals move the same way, back and forth, an occasional glance out of the bars, and then back to the mindless pacing.

"Easy for you to say. Don't you realize there's a railroad to lose if we don't beat Parsons across the divide? Damnation!"

Slocum knew better than to say anything. He sat quietly and, after a few minutes of futile effort, Melody gave up trying to pacify her father and came to sit beside Slocum. He was aware of the warmth of her leg against his. He tried to move away, but the woman followed him, her thigh rubbing slightly against his.

"Slocum," Bergstrom said. Slocum jumped. His mind had been on Melody. "Get that good-for-nothing agent

Ellis the instant we stop in Denver. I've got another train waiting to take the goods back to the base camp. When it arrives, there ought to be enough progress on repairing the rails farther up toward Widowmaker Pass that we can just keep moving it up where it's needed."

"Yes, sir," Slocum said. He stood to get away from Melody. She was asking for trouble and didn't seem to notice. "Count on me."

"I do, Slocum. You're a good man." Bergstrom continued pacing, hands clasped behind his back. Twenty minutes later the train screeched to a halt. Slocum was already swinging off the engine and dropping onto the platform before the train came to a complete halt.

"Need to find Ellis," he called to the stationmaster. "Know where I can find him?"

"Ellis? Saw him a bit earlier. Him and another guy went around back. He might be in the outhouse. If he is, I'd recommend you wait a spell. That man creates such a godawful stink you'd think he—" The stationmaster bit off the rest of his sentence as a thin, weasely man rounded the corner.

"Mr. Ellis?" asked Slocum.

"Who wants to know?" Squinty eyes tried to focus on Slocum and failed. The dark eyes were centered in a sea of bloodshot, as if Ellis had been out celebrating all night long.

"Bergstrom's hot to get the order placed. He wants the supplies out as quick as possible."

"Humph." Ellis pushed past Slocum, not even bothering to reply. The thin man climbed into Bergstrom's coach and went in search of the railroad magnate. Slocum followed, curious about the agent. Something about him rankled, and it was more than his attitude. Slocum didn't have to like a man to respect him, but there was something of the sneak thief to Ellis. Slocum had seen drummers he trusted more.

"So get it done," raged Bergstrom. "What the hell am I paying you for, Ellis?"

"Please, Mr. Bergstrom, it's not that way." The agent shifted nervously from foot to foot, as if he was a young boy caught with his hand in the cookie jar. Slocum settled down to listen. He was glad Melody had returned to her own car; it kept him from diverting his attention between her and the agent.

"What way is it? I hired you to get supplies and now you tell me there's none to be had in all of Denver? This is a big town. Find my rails, find my foodstuffs!"

"The rails are easy enough to come by," Ellis said. "The steel mills down in Pueblo are turning out quality material. It's the other. Th-there's something of a shortage."

"Shortage? We're in harvest season!"

"Bad harvest," Ellis said.

"Not that I saw," Slocum cut in. "I rode across the eastern Colorado plains and the wheat crop was about the best I'd seen in years. Ranchers were happy that they were able to feed their cattle on grain before moving them along to the slaughterhouses, too."

Ellis shot him a cold look and turned back to Bergstrom. "I can get you top quality provender, but it's going to cost more."

"Damn the cost. But it'll come out of your commission. We have a contract, and you're not reneging on it."

Slocum knew what any reputable agent would do then. He'd argue, threaten to take Bergstrom to court, maybe try getting better terms. Ellis did none of this.

"Yes, sir, I know. I'll get a shipment ready to leave by ten this evening."

"You know where the freight train is. I'll check it out before sending it on its way. I'll remain in Denver for another few days on other business."

Ellis nodded and left. Slocum watched the thin man leave, puzzled at his sudden acquiescence. He had caved in when most men would have fought. Considering how he had tried to jack Bergstrom around on the price, this struck Slocum as peculiar. Bergstrom grumbled to himself and made endless calculations of how much he could afford. Slocum slipped from the car, intent on Ellis.

The agent hit the platform at a quick walk and never slowed. Slocum trailed him at a discreet distance, noting that Ellis didn't seem much worried that his business might be learned by anyone else. He turned suddenly into an alley and walked away from the rail yards. Slocum had to dodge about; following down the long, narrow alley was a sure way of being seen, but he had guessed the man's destination well.

Slocum came out in the narrow street just north of Larrimer Square still hot on Ellis's trail. The man stopped abruptly, looked up and down the street as if checking for anyone following him, then ducked into the building behind him.

Caught in the open, Slocum could do nothing but keep walking. If he had broken stride, he would have attracted attention to himself. But Ellis wasn't thorough enough. Slocum avoided detection and stopped in front of the building, a crooked smile coming to his lips.

Rocky Mountain Rail Line the sign in the window proclaimed. Slocum peered through the front window and saw Ellis vanishing into a rear office. Slocum walked to the side of the building. There weren't any convenient windows to look through here, but he didn't need any. The walls were thin and not well constructed.

Hunkering down and pressing his ear to the wall, Slocum heard what went on in the office.

"—well done, Mr. Ellis."

"Glad you think so, Mr. Parsons. I'll be sure to earn this, I will, sir!"

"You've always come through for me before," Parsons said. "I see no reason to think this time will be any different." There was a long pause, then Parsons added, "But if there's any trouble, it'll be your neck. This isn't a game any longer. It's a damned war!"

"War, sir?"

"If so much as one piece of moldy bread reaches Bergstrom's men, I'll flay you alive."

"I understand, sir. There won't be any problem. I promise."

Slocum returned to the street and waited just around the corner of the building. In a few minutes Ellis came out, wiping sweat from his narrow forehead. He was the picture of nervousness, fidgeting and unsure of himself. The agent made up his mind and rushed off, almost catching Slocum off guard. He pressed back against the building and let Ellis pass within five feet. The thin agent was so intent on his mission that he didn't see Slocum.

The man hurried along to a purchasing office four blocks away from Parsons's office. Slocum walked past slowly, seeing who Ellis spoke with inside. The balding man that came boiling from the office had to be Ellis's assistant from the way he bolted when spoken to. Slocum considered staying with Ellis, then decided against it. He was supposed to be out hunting up a doctor to look at his injuries, but he was feeling good. He had been shot up worse than this during the war and had never needed a doctor's skill.

Something told Slocum that following the bald man was more important than having a few scratches marked up with iodine.

The bald man stopped at several warehouses and issued orders, pointing, shouting, and making sure his bidding was carried out as fast as possible. Slocum tried to decide what was happening and couldn't. If anything, it seemed Ellis had built a fire under his assistant to be sure Bergstrom's goods were delivered. Two dozen men worked like slaves to load crates onto the beds of heavy freight wagons. In less than a half hour, they were on their way to the rail yard, the bald man riding high in the driver's box.

Slocum wondered what the hell was going on. Bergstrom's supplies were being loaded. He didn't doubt the heavy steel rails would come from the Pueblo foundries on their own cars, which would be transferred to Bergstrom's engine. There wasn't any need to unload and reload such heavy freight.

Slocum checked to be sure the boxes were being loaded into the right warehouses. Less than a hundred yards away was the siding with the waiting freight cars. Slocum guessed Bergstrom would have to check out the crates before being loaded. The siding was clearly marked with a sign stating the freight cars were the property of the Denver and Utah Railroad, so there wouldn't be any trouble finding the right train after dark. He walked around and saw that the next siding had a similar sign, but this one stored the narrow-gage cars of the Rocky Mountain Rail Line. Scratching his chin, Slocum found a spot in the shade and went to sit and think.

Bergstrom had his supplies loaded into the padlocked warehouse and ready to go in record time. All that was needed was to transfer the crates from the warehouse. The flatbed cars carrying the heavy rails would be hooked on later in the day when they arrived from down south. So what had Ellis seen Anthony Parsons about? It had been clear to Slocum that the agent was being bought off. He was supposed to delay Clarence Bergstrom's food shipment as long as possible, yet he seemed to be expediting it.

Heaving himself to his feet, Slocum followed the bald man down the street and into a saloon.

"Gimme a shot," the bald man called out. The barkeep dropped a glass on the bar and had it filled before the man reached it. The bald man knocked it back, heaved a deep sigh of satisfaction, then asked for another.

"Ellis still working you to an early grave?" the barkeep asked.

"The man's a slave driver, he is," the bald man answered.

"Don't worry about him none, Joe. You got a good crew."

"I got a good crew, but he asks for the damnedest things. It's always run here, run there. Everything's a rush with Ellis. I swear he'll be ten minutes early for his own funeral, just to be sure everything's loaded right."

"What were you loading this time?"

Slocum's ears pricked up for the answer.

"Women's clothing. I swear, I didn't know there was so many womenfolk over there on the western slope. We must have loaded two dozen crates of women's clothing for the Denver and Utah warehouse."

"Didn't know they'd got through Widowmaker Pass yet. What about Parsons and his crew?"

Joe shook his shining head. "Can't rightly say, but they must be still at it. Ellis had us load up a warehouse down at the yards for them last night. They're waiting for more rail, too, just like Bergstrom."

"Women's clothes and steel rails. Don't make sense, does it?" the barkeep asked.

"I just do what I'm told. Lemme have another."

Slocum didn't wait for the barkeep to get to him. He turned and walked from the saloon, his mind racing. Ellis had ordered crates of clothing put onto Bergstrom's freight cars. Somehow the notion of the burly Irish workers wearing women's clothes struck Slocum as funny. But when he'd stopped laughing, he knew what had to be done. But it would be a while before he could act. Until then, he decided he'd better find a doctor and have his shoulder looked at. It was getting a mite stiff again, though that might have come from Melody sleeping on it most of the night when they weren't making love.

It was just after sundown when Slocum returned to the rail yard. He sauntered over and casually pulled the sign up declaring this was the Denver and Utah siding. He tucked the sign under his arm and kept walking until he came to the one for the Rocky Mountain Rail Line. A quick switch and he returned to Bergstrom's siding, planting the sign for Parsons's railroad.

"Hey, what you doin' there, mister?" came a bull-throated roar. "You ain't supposed to be nosin' around here. It's dangerous. You might get your legs chopped off or something."

"I was trying to figure out who got everything so mixed up that it'd take a month of Sundays to get straight," Slocum said. "I work for Mr. Parsons," he lied, "and you got the signs backwards."

"What? No, we couldn't have. I—"

Slocum went over to the man, looked up at him and shoved his face closer. The man moved away just enough to let Slocum know he had the upper hand now.

"You were trying to put freight on a train designed for narrow gage. I don't know where you got that notion that it was all right to do that."

"Narrow gage? But it's standard down here. It don't switch over to narrow till you get to the foothills."

"The size is different," Slocum insisted. "It's a good thing I got it right, or you'd been putting all the freight on the wrong train. I just saved you one royal whaling. You know how Mr. Parsons gets." Slocum coughed and added in a lower voice, "You heard what he did to Ellis, didn't you? A real shame about him."

"What went on? I knew Ellis was takin' money from him. That wasn't right, and I told him he shouldn't be in Bergstrom's pay, too."

Slocum spat. "That's for Bergstrom. I just want to make sure the food and other supplies get loaded proper-like."

"Yes, sir, right away," the huge man said. He stopped, turned, and scratched his head. "That train?" he asked, pointing to Bergstrom's freight cars.

"That's Mr. Parsons's," Slocum said, relishing the lie. "Get that food loaded on quick, and go on and load the crates of clothing on Bergstrom's train while you're at it. I'll stand the lot of you to a drink if you get it finished within the hour."

"Done!" the man cried, anxious for the drink and to prove himself to Anthony Parsons's supposed henchman.

Slocum watched impassively as the foodstuffs were loaded onto Bergstrom's train and the crates of women's clothing were shoved unto the boxcars on Parsons's siding. Now and then the crew's supervisor took a curious look at the signs Slocum had switched, as if not believing them. Then he'd look at Slocum and yell at his men to keep working. It took less than an hour to get Bergstrom's supplies stashed properly.

"There's the shipment of rail from Pueblo," the supervisor said. "Should we go on and hitch up the train?"

"Do it," Slocum said. He recognized the Denver and Utah insignia on the side of the engine backing into the siding and locking firmly onto the lead freight car. In less than ten minutes it was pulling out.

"That sure as hell looked like we put the wrong freight in the wrong train," the supervisor said, still frowning and looking at the signs Slocum had switched.

"Why, I do believe you're right," Slocum said, going over and moving the signs back the way they had been. "You think you ought to go on over to the Rocky Mountain Rail Line office and tell Mr. Parsons you loaded his supplies onto the wrong train?"

The supervisor paled.

"Don't worry about it," Slocum said. "If Ellis or anyone in Parsons's office asks, tell them Slocum said it was all right. Now, I promised your crew a drink, and I'm a man of my word. Pick your saloon, then pick your poison."

The supervisor smiled weakly, then yelled for his men to join them. Slocum slipped away after an hour of drink-buying. It was worth it to him knowing Bergstrom's supplies were well on their way to Widowmaker Pass and that Emmett Wall would have nothing but a dozen crates of women's clothes to pass out to his railroad crew.

13

Pleased with his nefarious handiwork, Slocum made his way to the hotel just off Oak Street where the Bergstroms had registered. He was supposed to stay with the posh sleeping cars on the siding, but he doubted Parsons would try anything there. He had already been thwarted and any revenge he might try to take would come in another form. Blowing up a sleeping car did nothing to keep the Denver and Utah from completing its line across Widowmaker Pass.

In the hotel lobby he saw Melody sitting at an ornate writing desk and penning a letter. He went to her. She looked up just as he took off his hat.

"John! I was so worried. What happened to you?"

"Been doing a job for Anthony Parsons," he said. He enjoyed the way her eyes turned round and a horrified expression crossed her pretty face. She started to say something, but no words came out.

"This is about the first time I've ever seen you speechless," Slocum said, smiling.

"But you said—"

"Seems Mr. Parsons got the notion into his head to bribe your agent."

"Ellis? But he's worked for Papa for more than three years. He's a strange man but not dishonest."

"He's crookeder than a dog's hind leg," Slocum declared. "I saw him in Parsons's office taking a bribe to load worthless material onto your freight cars."

"Worthless? But what could that be? We need most all types of supplies."

"Ladies garments," Slocum said. "He was to load a couple dozen crates of clothing in place of your food."

"What happened? You said you were doing a job for Parsons."

"I was overseeing the loading. Seems Parsons got what he bought through Ellis. It's on its way up to Grand Gorge right now. Twenty-four cases of dresses."

"And the food?"

"Seems that got put onto a Denver and Utah train bound for Widowmaker Pass. In spite of their conniving, everything's right."

"Oh, John, what would we do without you?" She jumped up and threw her arms around his neck and kissed him. In a lower voice she asked, "What would *I* do without you?"

Slocum didn't have much of an answer for that. He disengaged from her grip. It wasn't fitting for a proper woman to kiss a man in public, much less one working for her father.

"Who are you writing?" he asked.

"Just making an entry into my diary. I keep it every night, but everything I'm putting in has been getting boring."

"Boring?" Slocum asked. "After what I've told you about Ellis and Parsons?"

"Oh, yes, boring. I only enter those things of a personal nature. There is no need to keep a record of business doings. And it is getting boring sitting around this dreary hotel with nothing to do."

Slocum looked around. This might not be the Palmer House, but it was hardly dreary. It was a well appointed hotel with a liveried staff, fine carpets on the floors, highly polished wood everywhere he looked, and tasteful oil paintings on the walls. He wasn't much inclined toward the fancy artwork, but he recognized it as the sort of thing rich people enjoyed.

"I agree," Melody said softly. "About the artwork. I saw the way you stared at it, that one painting in particular. I also prefer something more like you'd find behind a bar."

"What?"

"Come now, John. I haven't led a sheltered life. Papa's not been rich all my life. He's made and lost three or four fortunes. If he loses again with the railroad, well, he'll start over. While I can't say I grew up in a saloon, I have spent some time there." In a lower voice still, she added, "And I enjoy the atmosphere."

Slocum had to laugh. This kind of low taste was the last thing he expected from Melody Bergstrom. She was one continual surprise for him, always catching him off guard with the unexpected things she said and did. He liked that.

"Take me to some of the Denver clubs. You must know where we could sample the nightlife. It is so lonely up there on the mountain. And there aren't many people I can talk to in Central City."

"I can appreciate that," Slocum said. There wasn't a young woman within fifty miles of Central City that could hold a candle to Melody Bergstrom. Working in the midst of a crew of Irish roughnecks wasn't the best life for her, either. But he held back offering to take her to the clubs he knew in the city. Many of them were exclusively for men. Others were too uncouth for a woman like Melody, no matter what she said.

"You do know of a few spots where we can go?"

"What are you interested in?"

"Some gambling, perhaps. I know I couldn't sit in, but I'd like to watch you play. I suspect you are a good player."

"What makes you say that?" Slocum asked.

"Gus told me how you came to work for the Denver and Utah."

"And?" Slocum prodded. "I lost that hand."

"Gus is a terrible player, but he knows a losing hand from a winning one. You could have taken his money and ridden off, but you didn't. You told him you lost when you'd won with a flush."

"Seems as if there are no secrets left anywhere in the world," Slocum said, marveling that Maguire had caught on to the deception—and that he had told Melody.

"Do take me to a few clubs, John. Please, please!"

He wasn't going to deny her. He was hardly dressed for the poshest of the clubs, but he knew one or two where he might get into a decent poker game and where Melody wouldn't be out of place. Slocum held out his arm for her. She took it quickly.

Together they walked the streets around Larrimer Square, then took a side street away from the gaslit section. Slocum studied the silent, barred doors lining the street until he saw one with a small red X above it. The clubs came and went quickly, sometimes moving after only a day's operation. The mark showed former patrons the new location.

Slocum rapped on the door, which opened a fraction. He saw a huge dark figure just beyond and a single watery eye peering out at him. Slocum said nothing, and the man inside said nothing. After a few seconds of scrutiny, the man opened the door a bit wider and motioned with his head that Slocum should enter.

Melody almost squealed with glee. Slocum wondered at her notion of entertainment. The room was smoky, and pretty girls moved from table to table selling drinks and themselves.

"John, they're hardly wearing anything at all!" Melody exclaimed.

"Stay close. The manager has a reputation for recruiting among patrons."

"No!"

Slocum wondered if she was going to bruise his arm. Her strong fingers clamped down like steel bands as she moved a little closer. He didn't have to warn her not to wander off; getting her pried free of his arm was going to take a crowbar.

"Lookin' for a game, mister?" asked a small ratlike man at a table. Slocum looked him over and saw all the accoutrements of a cardsharp. The man hadn't even bothered properly hiding the card holder in his sleeve. Under the eyeshades he wore was a large dark spot that might hold a card; all he had to do was adjust the shade and a new card would be in his hand. And the shining ring on his left hand reflected enough for Slocum to know the man could deal a card and see it in the metal. This wasn't the game for him, unless he wanted to finish it by shooting a card cheat.

Slocum shook his head and kept walking.

"What was wrong with that man?" Melody asked. "He wanted to play."

"No, he didn't want to play," Slocum answered. "He wanted to cheat. I prefer playing the odds dictated by the cards, not the dealer."

He watched two more games while Melody rubbernecked and took in everything in what, for her, was an illicit establishment. She couldn't keep her eyes off the pretty waitresses and their skimpy costumes. Now and again one would leave with a well-heeled customer and vanish down a narrow corridor, going back to the cribs for a quick tumble. Slocum was pleased that Melody knew enough that she didn't ask where the women and their patrons were going.

"This one," he said. "It's as close to honest as there is here." He sat in an empty chair and pulled out his meager stake. He had been spending freely on Maguire's crew and on the bald man's workers and had little enough left.

"That's all you got, mister?" the man across from him asked. "That's hardly enough for one hand."

"It's enough if I win," Slocum said. He looked around the table, estimating his chances. With these men it was fairly good. They had the look of players who enjoyed the game and didn't much care about odds. The thrill of taking a pot mattered more than how much they lost during the rest of their play.

"John, if you need more," Melody started, reaching into her purse. His hand clamped on her wrist.

"Don't go flashing a wad of money here, even if it's nothing but greenbacks. The place is honest only to a point."

"Oh," she said. He saw the combination of fear and excitement on her face. He wondered about Melody, but he wasn't going to question what got her excited. After he finished with the poker, he knew she'd be hotter than a pistol. On the train to Denver, she had damned near worn him out. But tonight would be even better. He saw it from the flush in her cheeks and the way she trembled.

Slocum played cautiously, losing only a small amount in the first two hands. Then he began betting seriously and started winning. After ninety minutes, he had won fifty dollars.

And, from the way Melody Bergstrom clung to him, he'd be a winner in ways other than money when they got back to her hotel.

"Time to fold up, gents," Slocum said after he'd lost a small hand. He had learned it never paid to leave a game having won. That made the others testy. This way he could always plead the beginning of a losing streak, something all gamblers would appreciate.

Slocum was glad to see that the others didn't mind him walking away with some of their money. With Melody clinging tightly, they left the club, passing the huge bouncer on the way out.

"That was thrilling, John. I've never been in such a place. And those poor women! Why, they were wantonly selling themselves to the customers!"

"More than that," Slocum said. "They were selling themselves and giving most of the money to the man who owns the club." He felt a shiver of delicious danger course through Melody.

It was going to be one hell of an evening once they got back to her hotel.

They hurried directly back, both of their imaginations running wild. Slocum had done a decent night's work, getting the supplies on their way to Maguire up at the construction camp. He had set back Anthony Parsons's schedule for a spell, and now he was going to cap it off with a passionate night with Melody Bergstrom. He couldn't ask any more from life.

"Oh, John, thank you for this evening. It—it was better than anything else I've ever done!"

She stood on tiptoe and kissed him with all the fervor locked inside. Slocum couldn't resist returning the kiss. And he couldn't miss the angry roar that shattered the stillness in the hotel lobby.

"What the hell are you doing with my daughter, Slocum?"

Slocum spun around, still holding Melody. He saw Clarence Bergstrom storming down the broad stairs.

"Mr. Bergstrom, I just—"

"You just nothing!" bellowed Bergstrom. "How dare you take advantage of her?"

"Papa, it isn't that way."

"Silence!" the railroad magnate shouted. "You won't start whoring around with hired help. Get to your room."

"But, Papa, I—"

Bergstrom started to hit his daughter. Slocum moved to stop the man, and the motion caused Bergstrom's anger to shift focus. He glared at Slocum, his jaw clenched.

"And you, Slocum, you're fired. Get the hell out of my sight. I swear if I see you sniffing around my daughter again, I'll load your worthless hide with buckshot!"

Bergstrom grabbed Melody's arm and spun her around, dragging her up the stairs. Slocum stood and watched, wondering what had gone wrong so fast to ruin his perfect evening.

14

Slocum tried to protest, but Clarence Bergstrom wouldn't listen. The man stormed up the broad flight of stairs, Melody trailing behind him and trying to talk some sense into the man. Slocum shook his head. Kissing the woman in public wasn't a good idea. It wasn't proper and just wasn't done in polite company, but Slocum thought he deserved more than summary firing for the minor offense.

A small smile wrinkled the corners of his mouth. Bergstrom would find that shotgun if he ever found out how his daughter and Slocum had spent their time on the way to Denver. That didn't make the firing any less galling, though.

Slocum had done good work for the Denver and Utah Railroad, and this was the thanks he got for it. He spun and stalked out, growing angrier by the minute. Such ingratitude rankled, but there wasn't anything he could do about it. Bergstrom was the owner of the railroad and could hire and fire as he saw fit.

Returning to the sleeping cars, Slocum went inside and made a quick check to be sure nothing out of the ordinary had occurred. Parsons might not find out about the switch in cargo for hours, maybe not until the freight arrived at his

Grand Gorge camp. That suited Slocum just fine and gave him a chance for a good night's sleep.

He sprawled across Melody's bed, the soft fragrance rising up to remind him of her perfume and the time they had spent here. It took some time, but Slocum finally drifted off to a troubled sleep.

He awoke with the sun in his face and a loud banging at the car's far door. His hand flashed to his cross-draw holster and pulled the six-shooter, ready for a fight

"John Slocum, you in there? Open up! This is Deputy Fulton."

The banging continued until Slocum thought they were going to break the door down. When a crack appeared in the beveled glass, Slocum decided he ought to see what the ruckus was all about, deputy or no deputy. He slipped out the other door but didn't step into Clarence Bergstrom's personal coach. He swung up and got onto the roof of Melody's car, then walked slowly to the rear.

"We got him penned up," one man said.

"I don't want him penned up here, I want him in the goldanged jail!"

Slocum didn't have to look to know this was the deputy speaking. He dropped to his belly and peered over the edge. He caught his breath. This wasn't just any deputy. This was No-Ear Fulton, a lawman as likely to bring his man back dead as alive. From all the stories Slocum had heard about Fulton, the man preferred dead, because that way his prisoners didn't put up any fuss. Fulton wore a blood-red patch where his left ear had been.

Slocum wasn't sure how the lawman had lost the ear. One story held that Fulton had shot it off as a dare. Slocum had also heard that a grizzly bit it off before Fulton returned the honor and bit the bear's ear off. It didn't much matter how the mutilation had happened. Slocum faced one ornery cayuse.

"Get on out of there, Slocum. We got a warrant for you sworn out by Clarence Bergstrom. We just want to get you out of town. Ain't nothing personal in this," Fulton finished insincerely, as if this lie would entice Slocum out.

A clatter from inside made Slocum tense. The back door had been kicked in. Heavy footfalls sounded and then the door just below him swung open. He blinked when he saw how fast the lawman got his six-shooter from its holster.

"Watch yourself, you fool. I coulda shot you down," Fulton said, putting his gun back into its holster. "Where's Slocum?"

"Ain't here. Looks as if he spent the night, but he's gone now."

"Was the bed warm?" Fulton saw no answer was forthcoming and pushed past his assistant. Slocum lay flat, thinking hard. His roan, saddle, and other gear were still back at the Denver and Utah camp. He'd need a way of getting to the camp if he wanted to retrieve them.

"Can't see how long he's gone. Damn him. Bergstrom is going to be mad at this." Fulton stood just under Slocum, hands on his hips, his head moving slowly to take in the entire rail yard. "Get on out there, men, and find him. He can't be far off."

"Why's that?" someone asked.

"Because I feel it in my gut, that's why. Move!" Fulton made to kick the deputy balking at the hunt. The man scuttled like a crab and took off. The other three deputies with Fulton didn't need any such encouragement. Slocum watched them fan out while Fulton remained below him. Slocum considered jumping the lawman, then discarded the notion.

No-Ear Fulton was *fast*.

Slocum lay flat and let the rising sun warm his body. The aches he had accumulated over the past week were mostly memory now, but he wished he could get away. Almost an hour later the deputies returned. Only then did Fulton agree to carry the search back into Denver. Slocum watched them leave, wondering what Clarence Bergstrom had told them to make them so intent on throwing him in jail.

Swinging down over the edge of the car's roof, Slocum dropped to the ground. He wondered how many trains were heading west. He could catch a ride on one of them and get to the junction splitting off from the northern route and the one still being laid over the divide. This meant he might have to hike a few miles, but it was better than staying in Denver.

Two trains were readying for departure. Slocum saw that one belonged to the Rocky Mountain Rail Line. He discarded the idea of stowing away on this train. It was going in the general direction he wanted, but getting caught aboard it might be fatal. The other train was a heavy freight train laden with goods bound for Salt Lake City across the northern high pass route. This would do him, he decided, though he didn't look forward to a long walk to fetch his gear.

As he started for the freight train, he heard a sound that turned him to ice inside. Hammers were being pulled back; guns cocked and he felt the sights centering on his spine. From instinct more than anything else, Slocum dived forward and started rolling, hoping to reach a stack of crates before he got cut down.

Bullets ripped through the air where he had been a fraction of a second before. More bullets followed him, sending splinters from the crates in all directions. He spun around and put his back to the box as slugs tore through the air over his head.

"That's him, boys. Parsons put a hundred dollar reward on his head—and he don't care if he's dead or alive."

Slocum didn't recognize the voice, but he knew these weren't Fulton's deputies. He had run afoul of Anthony Parsons's men. For the first time this morning he wished he had been captured by the lawman. Fulton had a bad reputation but wasn't likely to cut down a man who surrendered peacefully.

"Circle him, get in on the sides, then fill him full of holes!" came the gloating command.

Slocum knew he couldn't stay where he was. He had his Colt Navy and three loaded cylinders in his pockets. That didn't permit a lengthy gunfight with either the law or Parsons's men. Looking around didn't give him any easy way out, so he began looking at the ground. It was hard packed but he saw the hint of a hole under a crate that gave him a surge of optimism about his future.

Pushing the crate aside, he saw a small depression caused by the continual dripping of water and the work of burrowing rats. Slocum had no time to be fussy about his new neighbors. A rat chittered at him and flashed baleful eyes in his direction. Slocum kicked at the huge animal, sending it scuttling off. He wasted no time wiggling under the crate, but when he got there, he found he didn't have the strength or the leverage to move the large box back into position. Struggling wildly, he tried to enlarge the small space and keep from being seen.

Above he heard another flight of bullets ripping at the crate. The vibrations came down to him and told him he was buzzard bait if Parsons's men caught him now. He twisted around so he could look out under the crate. He saw boots moving just inches from his face. He clutched his Colt Navy, worrying that the mud might have fouled the mechanism.

"Where'd he go? He just upped and vanished like a puff of smoke."

Others chimed in with their opinions. Whoever led the band shouted new orders and sent them rushing off into the rail yards. From his vantage point, Slocum craned his neck and saw a train slowly pulling out along a siding. He squirmed a bit to get a better look, then ducked back into his hiding place when Parsons's men came back looking for him.

He cursed his bad luck. He couldn't tell which train was pulling out. It might be the freight train going on to Salt Lake. If so, that was the one he had to be on. Missing his chance meant staying in Denver for long hours. He wasn't sure he could elude both the law and Parsons's gunmen that long. He had been lucky so far, but luck had a nasty way of turning when he needed it most.

"Back to the warehouse. I saw somebody ducking in there!" went up the cry. The sound of boots hitting the hard ground gave Slocum hope again. He corkscrewed himself out from under the crate and looked around. Parsons's men circled a warehouse not ten yards away. Moving as quietly as he could, Slocum stood, turned, and walked off.

The hair on the back of his neck rose. Every step he took might carry with it a bullet to the spine. He kept walking until he crossed the tracks and was near the Salt Lake City freight train. He wanted to run, but to do that might attract attention. He had been lucky this far.

And, as he had feared, his luck vanished like dew in the hot morning sun. Someone spotted him and shouted, "There he is! A hundred dollars to the man who cuts him down!"

Slocum looked over his shoulder and saw men boiling out of the warehouse. Lead began flying again. He fired wildly at them, not trying to aim. He just wanted to drive them to cover, and for a few lucky seconds, it worked.

Then he found himself dashing in front of the freight train, the engineer blowing the whistle and shouting angrily at him. Slocum waved to the man and tried to show he was sorry that he had almost been run over, but it was a false apology. The train cut off the cloud of bullets seeking his hide and gave him a chance to decide what to do next.

"I wanted to get on this train," Slocum said, thinking out loud, "so why not do it?"

He jumped, catching a metal rung on the side of a freight car. He swung between cars and pressed his body flat to keep from being seen. A few bullets came his way, but he didn't think anyone had spotted him. It wouldn't have mattered if they had; the engineer was pulling out come hell or high water.

The train rattled and clanked through the rail yard and finally reached the outskirts of Denver. Like a dose of smelling salts, Slocum felt the reviving fresh air against his face. He sucked in a huge draught of air and let it out slowly. He was free of Denver and on his way back to Widowmaker Pass.

Getting his horse, gear, and back pay wouldn't take more than a few minutes. Then he would be free of Bergstrom, Parsons, the crazy race across the divide—and Melody.

15

Slocum got careless when the train screeched to a stop forty miles outside Denver. He rode on the top of the last freight car and didn't duck down in time to keep from being seen when the oiler and engineer climbed onto the water tower to refill the train's boiler. The engineer spotted him and fifteen minutes later Slocum found himself sitting beside the tracks watching the train puff and strain as it left the small station.

He looked up and saw that the name of the town was Forlorn Junction. It seemed about the most aptly named place he had ever been stranded. He touched his left shirt pocket with his poker winnings from the night before and wondered if this miserable hole had a livery or anyone willing to sell him a horse.

An hour later he found the answer to that. No one in town wanted to part with their animals at any price. One man looked longingly at the wad of greenbacks Slocum flashed, but even the full hundred dollars wasn't enough to pry loose the promise of a sale of even a swaybacked nag. Forlorn Junction was too much off the beaten path for its handful of residents to give up animals vital to their survival.

"So when's the next train coming through?" Slocum asked the man doubling as stationmaster.

The old geezer scratched his stubbled chin, worked over a faded schedule turned yellow and brittle with age, and then shook his head. "Can't rightly say, but there's supposed to be a special through some time this afternoon. Doubt if it'll stop, though."

"How would you signal it to stop, if it's not planning to take on water?"

"Don't know. Problem's never come up before. Might put a sign out on the platform."

Slocum eyed the old man with some skepticism. A train barreling along wouldn't have the time to read the sign and stop, even if the sign was put a mile down the track. And he had heard of more than one enterprising road agent switching from stagecoaches to trains for a living. Unless something blocked the track, an engineer wasn't going to stop, and Slocum doubted any train man would take kindly to taking on a passenger who sabotaged his precious schedule.

"Do you have a telegraph? I can send a message to Denver and—"

"We got wires but no telegraph," the man said, bending almost double and looking out under the station house roof as if to make sure they were still there. He pointed to the wires. "The Denver and Utah strung 'em, they did, but they didn't bother giving us a telegraph key. Wouldn't matter much if they had."

"Why's that?"

"Ain't nobody in the Junction what knows Morse code."

Slocum saw he wasn't getting anywhere with the old man. He left and hiked toward Denver, thinking to flag down the special train coming through. Sitting on a rise, he chewed on a stalk of grass and stared at the empty horizon. When he saw a cloud of steam rising from the direction of Denver, he jumped to his feet. Getting the train to stop would be hard, but it beat walking.

Slocum went to the tracks and took off his vest to use as a flag. But the instant the train got close enough to make out details, he knew he was out of luck.

Clarence Bergstrom's personal train rumbled past, picking up speed as it hit a small downslope. Slocum didn't see either the railroad magnate or his daughter, but a lump formed in his throat.

Melody Bergstrom was one lovely woman, and Slocum had been treated poorly by her father. What was the harm in a small kiss, even if it had been in public? The anger rose within him again and didn't die down for hours.

He walked back to the station and sat under the water tower, wondering what he was going to do. Hiking into Widowmaker Pass wasn't possible, not if he wanted to reach there before the snows began falling. Slocum finally decided that the Denver and Utah wasn't the only train using this stretch of track. Another would be along, and one had to stop for water, as the freight had done.

He finally slipped aboard a train that stopped to take on water at dawn the next day. He didn't bother offering the conductor money for passage; Slocum took some small satisfaction in crawling up under the cars and finding a small bed of steel rods where he could lie. The ride was terrible, and he chipped a tooth as the train clacked and bounced along the track, but by noon he had reached the junction of this track with the Denver and Utah rails heading up into the mountains.

Dropping off, he stretched and tried to shake the kinks out of his cramped muscles. He looked around the junction and finally found what he had hoped to. The Denver and Utah ran back and forth along the stretch often enough to leave equipment at the junction. A handcar in good condition was exactly what Slocum needed. Fighting it onto the track took almost an hour. Two men could have done it quickly, but the grooved wheels refused to roll over the hard ground without digging ruts, and once Slocum wrestled it to the cindered railroad bed, he needed a second set of hands to lift the car onto the track.

He persevered and began the long, tedious, backbreaking work of pumping the handle up and down to get the handcar moving. Slowly at first, then with gathering speed, he moved along the section of Denver and Utah track. Once, in the distance, he saw the gleam of afternoon sun off a stretch of Rocky Mountain Rail Line narrow gage track. By sundown Slocum was ready to collapse.

The track was going up into the hills, making pumping more and more strenuous. Slocum kept at it until his belly started growling so loud he knew he couldn't go on much longer. Finding a level stretch, Slocum jumped off and went hunting. He bagged two rabbits, made a small fire, and dined better than he had in several days. Not about to take the handcar off the track, Slocum worried a little about a train rushing through and hitting it. Then he decided it wasn't his problem. Only Bergstrom's trains used this track—and Bergstrom owed him.

Slocum slipped into a fitful sleep, feeling the nighttime chill of the high country because of lack of a blanket. When morning came, he was stiff, sore, and not so sure he was inclined to keep pumping on the handcar. But he did. He had a horse to retrieve and back pay to collect. Not even Clarence Bergstrom could deny him what he had worked so hard to earn.

That thought kept him going all day long and into the short afternoon when he finally came to the Denver and Utah base camp. At first he thought they had pulled out in favor of the construction site farther along up in Widowmaker Pass. Then he saw the carnage that had been wreaked on the camp. For several seconds he just stared, unbelieving.

Parsons and Wall might consider themselves in a fight, but this looked as bad as anything Slocum had seen during the war. Tents burned and he heard the pitiful moans of injured men.

He jumped to the ground and went to see if it was as awful as it looked. It was. He knelt next to a man he knew and held his head up so he wouldn't choke on his own blood. Eyes fluttered and a broken-toothed grin showed through bloodied lips.

"Slocum, knew ye'd make it back. Bloody barstids did this."

"Who? Parsons?"

"Him and Wall and the others. He—they—" He said no more. He coughed once and slipped bonelessly from Slocum's grip. Slocum reached down and closed the man's unseeing eyes, then moved on. At least half a dozen men were severely injured. From the extent of their wounds, Slocum guessed that dynamite had gone off in the center of the camp while they had been eating.

He moved through the destroyed campsite, doing what he could for the injured. For the dead, there was nothing to be done. Slocum stopped and just stared when he saw one mangled body. Gus Maguire had never had a chance. Not only was a leg blown off, he had two bullet holes in his head.

Rage boiled inside Slocum. He had liked the short, bristly foreman. No government contract was worth this kind of butchery. Slocum moved on until he came to the siding where Bergstrom's fancy rail car was parked. Bullet holes in the sides told Slocum that one hell of a fight had been waged. The best he could figure, the dynamite had been planted and went off at mealtime, then Wall's gunmen had swarmed down and taken advantage of the confusion to shoot anyone still living.

Slocum swung up onto the car's rear platform. He pushed open the door and entered cautiously. Sobs greeted him. He touched his six-shooter, then saw it wouldn't be needed.

Clarence Bergstrom sat at his desk, ramrod stiff, tears running down his dirtied cheeks. A pistol lay on the desk near his hand and his clothing was ripped and bloodied. From the slow ooze in his chest he had caught at least one bullet high up. Slocum checked the man quickly and saw the blood was bright red; if it had been frothy pink there wouldn't have been any hope for the railroad owner.

"They took her. They came and took my daughter," he moaned.

"Parsons and Wall?"

"Yes, them. The whole lot came down and killed us where we stood. We never had a chance. I shot one, I think. They have Melody."

"How many of your crew is dead? Is anyone left in one piece?" Slocum asked, wondering if there was any way he could get a coherent story from the shocked man.

"He's always fancied her, he has. The son of a bitch! He has my daughter!"

"Parsons? You mean he's always had a liking for Melody?"

"I'd kill him but I can't move. My legs—"

Slocum moved the man back from the desk and saw that both of Bergstrom's legs had been shot up. Slocum wasn't sure what had happened, but it looked as if the kneecaps had been blasted to dust by more than a dozen bullets. Clarence Bergstrom would never walk again. How he got into his chair behind the desk was a mystery that would long go begging for an answer.

"Did you know Maguire was dead?" Slocum waved his hand in front of Bergstrom's face. The man had succumbed to shock and wasn't going to answer any questions. Slocum stepped back, then sat heavily in one of the luxuriously upholstered chairs. The way Bergstrom had treated him had been nothing short of criminal, but Slocum pushed that affront from his mind.

He still felt anger toward the railroad magnate, but there was a greater fury toward Parsons and Wall. They had killed innocent men, they had killed Gus Maguire, they had kidnapped Melody Bergstrom again.

Slocum wasn't going to let them get away with this. He stood and left the car, knowing there wasn't anything more he could do for Bergstrom. The man would either live or die, depending on his own inner strength. Getting his daughter back would do more to give him that courage to live than anything else Slocum could do.

16

Slocum found his horse and saddle. He checked the gear, made sure his Winchester was loaded and in good working condition, then got ready to ride. He worked with a sense of resignation that grew with every passing second. Anthony Parsons had kidnapped Melody before and only through a stroke of good luck had Slocum freed her. He didn't think Parsons—or Emmett Wall—would let him stroll in and out as he had done before. After the wreckage he had caused running the heavily loaded flatcars off the end of their flimsy trestle, that construction site would be heavily guarded. Just getting close to the camp without being seen would take all his skill.

As he rode toward the Rocky Mountain Rail Line camp, his resolve hardened. They shouldn't have killed Gus Maguire. He had been a good man, and Slocum had found too few of them in his travels. What they had done to Bergstrom was a crime, too, but Slocum couldn't find it in his heart to get as worked up over this. He had a grudge against Bergstrom, and he might have cut the man down if it had come to a shootout. But Parsons, or probably Wall, had crippled Bergstrom for life. That was despicable and hadn't been called for.

He neared the site and heard the sound of heavy hammers swinging and wood being sawed. Work still went forward on the trestle. Slocum wondered how much coal oil it would take for the entire bridge to be reduced to smoldering embers at the bottom of Grand Gorge. All he needed to do was find enough and put a lucifer to the oil-soaked wood. He usually didn't much enjoy watching something people had worked so hard to build go up in flames, but this time he'd make an exception.

A sixth sense told Slocum he was riding into danger. He bent forward, using his horse as a partial shield. The roan shied, but Slocum kept it under control. The bullet that whistled through the air seeking his heart told him he had been right to duck when he had. This time he let the horse bolt. Hitting him on a galloping horse from any great distance would be well nigh impossible, unless the bushwhacker was one hell of a good shot.

"There he goes. It's him, it's Slocum! Get him!" came the cry.

Slocum knew he had ridden into a den of sidewinders. It didn't much matter if they had been lying in wait for him or were interested in anyone coming into their camp. He veered off the road and took to the high country. His horse was rested and he made good time up the steep slope, but he knew he'd have every last one of Wall's killers on his trail. Parsons had put up a reward for him back in Denver.

This caused him to smile. He thought Parsons probably had found the shipping crates of women's clothing by now. Slocum hoped the railroad owner looked good in them.

He kept low as new slugs ripped above his head. The gunmen were shooting uphill and didn't have any idea how to aim. Most of the bullets fell short of their mark. By the time Slocum reached the summit, he had a good look at not only Parsons's camp but his pursuers.

He counted quickly and stopped when he got to ten. Any more than this was an army, and it didn't matter. The trestle was covered with coolies hammering, sawing, and fixing. Slocum saw evidence that the middle, where the flatcars had gone over, still hadn't been completely repaired. This made him think hard. Why was Parsons going to all this bother if the bridge was almost done? He had less than eight miles of track to lay over level terrain after the trestle was in place.

That meant the Rocky Mountain Rail Line wasn't as close to completion as it appeared. Something had come up to spook Parsons, and Slocum would have to capitalize on this if he wanted to come out with a whole skin—and Melody Bergstrom.

"Up the hill. Charge 'im. We can take him!"

Slocum dismounted and took his rifle from its saddle scabbard. He dropped to one knee, steadied himself, and waited. When he had a good shot, he took it. The long days as a sniper during the war paid off. His bullet didn't kill his target, but the man was wounded seriously enough to take him out of the fray. Even more to Slocum's liking, two others broke off the attack to help their fallen comrade. One bullet removed three attackers. Not bad.

Slocum kept up a slow, deadly fire that reduced the ranks of Wall's men further. Only when Emmett Wall himself put in an appearance did the tide turn against Slocum. He heard the foreman bellowing commands, getting his men back into a defensible position and prepared for a real attack.

"Sorry, old boy," Slocum said to his roan. "I've got to leave you. I don't think those sidewinders will hurt you, but you can never tell. They tried poisoning you once." Slocum rummaged through his saddlebags and got out all the spare ammunition he had brought. It was time for him to go hunting—or was it?

Slocum paused to look around again. The construction camp lay to the north. The attack came at him from the north and west. He had ridden up from the south. What lay to the east? What he saw convinced him a game of hound-and-hare wasn't in the cards. He wouldn't lead them around and wait for them to make a mistake. He'd hole up in one of the deserted mines he saw to the east and make them come in after him. It was dangerous because he might get penned up inside one of the spent shafts, but he thought his odds were better there.

They could only attack from one side at a time.

Slocum started for the nearest mine on foot. He heard shouts of anger fifteen minutes later when Wall got to the top of the rise and saw that his quarry had fled. Slocum had to wait long enough for Wall to look around and see him before ducking into the mine's gaping mouth.

Slocum studied the timbers; they seemed sturdy enough. He didn't want to get inside and have Wall decide simply to close the shaft, burying him alive. Slocum was counting on the foreman having nothing more than his side arm and a few rifles for armament. There wouldn't be much reason to come hunting with dynamite.

"All I have to do is remove them all before Wall sends back for some," Slocum said to himself. He hurried into the depths of the mine, then slowed as the light vanished. He groped around on the walls, hunting for a candle or torch. He found a miner's helmet with a carbide light on it. A few pebbles of carbide still rattled inside. All Slocum had to do was add water. He found a small river running down the center of the mine's floor that provided enough moisture to excite the carbide into a fitful light.

By this time Wall and the others had reached the mine's opening. Slocum turned, saw a silhouette, aimed, and fired in a smooth motion and was rewarded with a sick grunt. He had hit whoever it was exposing himself so foolishly. Slocum dropped to the floor, turned the carbide light toward a rock wall, and waited. Wall had control of the men, but he was impatient to be done with his hunt.

When Wall urged his men to enter the mine, Slocum shot two more, one directly and wounding the other with a chance ricochet. He made every shot count, even when a new barrage opened up over his head. Bullets sang their deadly paths into the empty mine. The echoes were deafening, but Slocum held his ground.

"You're trapped, Slocum. Come on out and we'll let you live," Wall shouted. "There's no way you can escape!"

Slocum knew that probably wasn't true. Wall's men would keep coming at him, and he would keep cutting them down until he ran out of ammo or they ran out of men. Slocum felt confident that he would be the victor in such a siege, but this wasn't enough for him. He had to get Melody Bergstrom back.

Putting on the battered tin miner's helmet, Slocum rolled over and got to his feet. He made his way deeper into the maze of spent tunnels. From the way the stopes went up, he guessed they had been looking for gold and had found only a few small veins. Sooner or later he'd find one of those chimneys that led to the surface; he wasn't more than fifty feet under the surface of the hill.

From behind, he heard argument. Wall tried to whip his men into a killing frenzy that would carry them deep into the mine after Slocum. The gunmen wanted no part of it. Slocum kept moving, hunting for the back door, the other way out of the mine. It might not exist, but Slocum thought that it did.

A few bullets banged into the rocks along the tunnel, but Slocum wasn't worried. He had made enough turns in the mine to protect his back. As he walked, he kept shining his light up at the ceiling. That was where the exit would be. Miners moved along on the level until they found a vein, then worked up, drilling and letting gravity pull the rock down around them. It saved having to haul the ore up from a pit.

Flashes of blue sky alerted Slocum that he had found his way out. He moved into the stope, studied it for a few seconds until he located the hand- and footholds cut in by some miner, then worked his way up. It took close to ten minutes before he heaved himself the final few feet and out onto the side of the hill. Below him stood several of Wall's men, milling about nervously and pointing into the mine.

Slocum measured the distance and started thinking about picking them off one by one. Before they could figure out where he was, he could remove all three men from the fight and effectively bottle up the others inside the mine. Then he saw another man struggling up the hill. This one carried a large wooden box.

Dynamite. Wall had decided to bury Slocum alive.

"That works both ways," Slocum said softly. He settled down and began firing. The first bullet took the man carrying the dynamite in the head. He flopped back and sprawled gracelessly on the ground not fifteen feet from the mouth of the mine shaft. Three more bullets killed another of Wall's henchmen and drove the other two into the mine for cover.

Sliding down the slope, firing occasionally to keep the men inside, Slocum dropped beside the mine's mouth. He had reversed positions with them, and he was just as cold-blooded as Wall.

Slocum ran to the fallen box of dynamite, got out some fuse and a blasting cap, then made his way back to the mine. He fired until his rifle ran empty, then switched to his Colt. Alternating a bullet with a few seconds' frenzied work finished his project and kept Wall's men penned up in the mine. He had the fuse and cap set in the middle of the dynamite crate.

He pushed it as far as he could into the mine, dropped to his belly, and crawled forward. Using the muzzle flash from his six-gun to light the black fuse let him put the bullet to good use. It raced into the mine and found a fleshy target in one of the pair who had taken cover.

"He's gonna blow up the mine. Rush 'im while we can!"

Slocum judged the length of fuse, decided he had less than thirty seconds left, and emptied his pistol at the men trying to race for freedom. He knocked out the empty cylinder, got a charged one, and slid it into his Colt Navy. That gave him six more shots, which he used quickly.

Ten seconds left on the fuse.

Slocum rolled out of the cave, fumbling for the third loaded cylinder. He didn't get it put into the pistol before the fuse detonated the dynamite. The explosion rocked the mountainside and a huge gout of dust and rock blasted from the mine.

Slocum ducked and was cut by only a few sharp flying stones. He shook his head to clear it, wondering if he had gone deaf. There was only total silence in the world. He looked up at the perfect blue sky and saw a large brown turkey buzzard circling lazily. It looked to be signaling others, but Slocum heard nothing. A curious ground squirrel poked its head up to see what had happened in the neighborhood and chittered loudly, but Slocum didn't hear it. He was deaf from the blast.

He was deaf and everyone in the mine was dead. Now it was time to fetch Melody.

17

Slocum wished he knew how many of Wall's killers he had trapped in the mine. However many it had been, it wasn't enough. Slocum wanted them all dead. Then he would take out Emmett Wall and finished with his boss, Anthony Parsons. Nothing less would satisfy him.

He hiked back to the top of the hill where he had left his horse. He found the roan grazing contentedly a few yards from where he'd left it. Slocum patted the horse and advised, "Get ready to ride like the wind. When I finish down there, I might need to make myself plenty scarce."

He didn't even want to consider failure. Gus Maguire's death would not go unavenged. Melody Bergstrom would not be left in Parsons's clutches. And the damned railroad would not cross the trestle. Slocum didn't care if he blew it up or burned it to the ground, but that bridge was becoming a symbol of all that was evil.

Slocum made his way down the hill, watered the roan at a small stream, then found a secluded area to tether the horse. He fumbled through his saddlebags and found what ammunition he had left. He reloaded the spare cylinders for his Colt and found enough extra ammo for the Winchester to put up a decent fight. Only then did he go hunting.

Slocum almost hoped he had trapped Wall in the mine shaft with his henchmen, but he had just begun to scout the camp when he heard faint cries. He dropped to one knee and tried to clear his ears. A tiny ringing noise bothered him, but he took this to be good news. His hearing was coming back after the explosion at the mine. Slocum waited until Emmett Wall's bellows sounded loud enough to give him some hope he would hear anyone sneaking up behind him.

"Consarn it, you lop-eared jackass!" shouted Wall. "What do you think you're doin'? I ought to kick your butt all the way back to China." Slocum watched as Wall beat one of the coolies who had dropped his end of a steel rail. Slocum was amazed that only two of the Celestials were needed to lug the heavy steel. Maguire always used three and sometimes four of his Irishmen on the track.

"Where's the rest of those fools? Haven't they got Slocum yet? Why do I have to do everything myself?" Wall ranted and raved and used a quirt liberally on whomever was closest. Slocum's trigger finger itched a mite when he considered the distance and how good a shot he had at the foreman. He decided against it when he saw the way the sun was sinking into the west and casting long, deceptive shadows. In the past, Slocum had missed what he thought were easy shots by misjudging where the body that formed such shadows actually stood. There would be time for Wall later, he decided.

Slocum skirted the camp. Several Chinese laborers saw him but said nothing. He didn't know if it just wasn't their way to get involved or if they understood he was bringing death to the men who worked them like slaves. He mingled with them, bent over so he wouldn't tower above the much shorter workmen. Slocum got to the edge of the bridge before he ducked behind a low bush, slipped and slid down a small incline, and ended up on a ledge ten feet below track level.

From this vantage point he could see the shoddy work that had been done on the trestle. It was about as he thought. Parsons had to shoot up Bergstrom and kidnap his daughter to slow the work on the Denver and Utah. Even with the prodigious task of getting through Widowmaker Pass, Bergstrom was going to beat Parsons to the other side of the divide. The first heavily laden train that tried to get across this bridge would end up in the river, alongside the two flatcars Slocum had already sent five hundred feet to their destruction.

He studied the underside of the bridge, guessing, evaluating, making plans. He needed some of the dynamite that had been wasted back in the mine shaft. Only a few sticks had been necessary to collapse the tunnel. The rest could have been used to wreck the trestle. Slocum consoled himself with the thought that there was more dynamite stashed around the camp. Wall needed it to blast out foundations for the bridge on either side of the gorge.

Slocum went to find the explosive, making his way up the slope. He dropped to his belly and watched in dismay as a buckboard and driver came rattling into camp. Slocum recognized the driver as one of Maguire's crew. The man jumped down from the buckboard and went around to the rear. Two more men rode there, shotguns resting in the crooks of their arms. Slocum couldn't see what else was in the wagon bed. He edged forward to get a better view.

Clarence Bergstrom was lifted from the wagon and lowered to the ground. One man hurried to set up a small campstool for the railroad baron. The pinched white face told Slocum Bergstrom was on the edge of death.

"Where's that son of a bitch Parsons?" Bergstrom roared in a surprisingly strong voice. "Get him out here."

"Well, well, lookee who we got comin' to pay us a visit." Wall tapped the quirt in his right hand against his left palm. He seemed to be estimating distances to see if he could lay it across Bergstrom's strained face.

Bergstrom glared at the foreman but said nothing. In a few minutes Anthony Parsons sauntered out, smoking a big cigar. The pungent blue smoke from the huge stogie caught the wind and rode past Slocum. His nostrils flared at the aroma. Seldom had he been treated to such a fine, rich smoke.

"Coming to pay me a visit, are we now, Clarence? I can't say the thought ever entered my mind to visit your camp."

"You sneaking, slimy, low-down, no-account—" Bergstrom sputtered out of breath.

"Is that any way to speak to the man who is going to take your most prized contract away from you? The Rocky Mountain Rail Line will be on the other side of the divide in less than a week. How are you coming across the pass?"

"I want her back. Name your price, but I want her back."

"Whatever are you talking about?" Parsons asked, his face glowing with a vicious sneer. "Could it be you're referring to your daughter? She's a pretty one, and feisty."

"Let her go and I'll do anything you want."

"Why should I?" Parsons circled the seated Bergstrom. "I don't see any competition from you. I've heard tell your foreman's upped and run off."

"Your men murdered him!"

"Such unfounded accusations, tut, tut," said Parsons mocking his rival. "As to your daughter, why, I do think she might want to marry me."

"Let her go and I'll stop all work. If you don't—"

"What will you do, cripple?"

Slocum saw Bergstrom try to stand. His legs wouldn't hold his weight any more. The man crashed back to the campstool. Bergstrom's fists tensed so much that his knuckles turned white and he shook as if he had the ague.

"I want her back, Parsons."

"So, maybe we can deal." Parsons puffed at his long cigar. In a voice too low to hear, he began talking to Bergstrom. From the man's reaction and that of the three men with him, Slocum knew what the deal entailed. The Denver and Utah had to stop work. When Anthony Parsons had the government reward all sewed up, he'd release Melody. Bergstrom slumped, as if he had lost all will to live. Then he lifted his gaunt face and nodded in agreement with Parsons's terms.

Parsons laughed, spun, and walked off, humming a jaunty air, enjoying his cigar. The men with Bergstrom loaded him back into the wagon and prepared to leave. Slocum scuttled around like a crab to stay low and not be seen. He had to talk to Bergstrom before the injured man got back to his camp or died. From the paleness, Slocum didn't think the man had too much longer to live.

Slocum paused and looked back into the Rocky Mountain Rail Line camp and considered just two shots, one for Wall and the other for Anthony Parsons. It would take only a few minutes and would get Bergstrom off the hook. Slocum rejected the idea when he considered that he hadn't seen hide nor hair of Melody. Parsons had her hidden somewhere, and she was in constant danger unless Slocum could rescue her. He didn't put it past Wall or Parsons to give orders to kill the woman if anything happened to either of them.

First he had to rescue Melody, then he would kill the two men.

Slocum made his way out of the camp, glad that there weren't any sentries posted. He had wiped out most of Wall's henchmen in the mine explosion. Those that remained were in the camp with their foreman. Slocum got to his horse and took the reluctant animal away from another patch of juicy green grass.

He put his heels to the animal's sides, asking it to give all it had. He wanted to catch Bergstrom before the man was bounced too far down the road. Riding in the bed of a buckboard was the closest thing to hell on earth Slocum had ever found. Bergstrom didn't have the constitution to tolerate it long.

He overtook the buckboard within ten minutes and waved them down. The men in the rear swung their shotguns around, then paused when they saw it was Slocum. They discussed the matter between themselves, then shouted to the driver to stop. Slocum pulled alongside and looked into the wagon. Bergstrom was even paler and breathing harshly.

"Mr. Bergstrom, you can't give in to Parsons like this," Slocum said.

"Why not?" Bergstrom croaked out. "I'm well nigh dead. Without Melody, what's the use of living?"

"Parsons is the one running scared. Why'd he make the raid on your base camp? Why'd he kidnap your daughter? Why'd he kill Maguire, unless he thought he was behind you? If you keep working, you can beat him to the other side of the Rockies."

"My daughter," Bergstrom croaked out. "She's more important than any railroad. I'd rather go bankrupt than lose her, too. She's so much like her beloved mother, so much."

"I can get her. If I return her to you, will you keep working on the railroad? You can beat Parsons!"

"What's this to you, Slocum? I fired you back in Denver. I'd've thought you be long gone by now."

"It's not just your daughter that keeps me involved," Slocum said. "Maguire was a friend. I don't let a friend's murder go unavenged."

"Don't do anything that will jeopardize Melody's life! I warn you!" Bergstrom coughed harshly and laid back in the wagon. His hand fluttered, indicating that the driver should continue.

"If I get her back, will you keep building the road?" Slocum repeated.

"Don't risk her life, Slocum. Don't. This is the way it has to be. It does. Parsons has won, damn him!" Bergstrom started coughing again. The driver snapped the reins and got the horses moving, pulling the buckboard up the steep slope leading back to the Denver and Utah base camp. Slocum watched them go, but he wasn't going to follow Bergstrom's orders. The man had been right. He had fired Slocum in Denver and that meant Slocum could do as he damn well pleased.

Slocum turned his horse and started back for Parsons's camp. He had serious work to do and it was getting dark.

18

Slocum knew it was dangerous going back to the same spot where he had tethered his horse before, but it had worked then. He decided it might work again and let him get into Parsons's camp without being seen. He found a new spot for his horse to graze, then set off on foot, carrying his rifle and a pocketful of spare ammo. The entire camp was abuzz with the news that Bergstrom had given up.

Anthony Parsons stood atop a large box of dynamite and shouted, "We've done it, men. I promised you a bonus when the work was done and we'd won. The work's a few weeks from completion, but the bonus will be given out next payday."

A huge cry of delight went up from Wall's henchmen. Slocum noted that the Chinese stood in small groups, talking among themselves. They hadn't been promised any bonus, Slocum was sure. They'd be lucky if they got a second bowl of rice for their backbreaking labor.

"The Denver and Utah is finished. They've quit construction because of insurmountable odds!"

Slocum's hand tensed on his rifle. It wouldn't be that difficult a shot to take out Parsons. He was bathed in light from the campfires. The shadows made it a trickier target than it would have been in broad daylight, but Slocum was considering it when he remembered his earlier thoughts. Parsons was the kind of man who would have left orders that Melody was to be killed if anything happened to him.

Slocum relaxed and lowered the rifle, hardly aware that he had been sighting in on Parsons. He had to find Melody, then he could worry about bringing retribution to the railroad baron.

He looked around the camp, wondering where Parsons might stash his kidnapped victim. There didn't seem to be any good place to hold the woman without everyone in camp knowing what had happened. Slocum doubted anyone would care, but from Parsons's words, most of the men didn't know the reason Clarence Bergstrom had given in to Parsons so easily. Wall and a few highly trusted gunmen must have made the raid on the Denver and Utah camp. As if verifying his guess, Slocum found Emmett Wall and four others standing at the edge of the crowd. They smirked, as if they shared a secret joke.

Would any of them know where Melody was being held captive? Slocum thought Wall knew, but the others? It was too risky to cut one of them from the herd and question him. Slocum had to keep telling himself he was surrounded by men willing to kill him and collect their hundred dollar reward.

Slocum moved back into shadow and turned toward the trestle. Something about it drew him. He went to the edge and looked out over it, considering his chances of destroying the entire structure, when he heard men coming behind him.

"I tell you, Emmett, it's too much trouble going all the way down there. Just let me stay there all the time. That way—"

"That way you can have your way with her. You know what Mr. Parsons thinks of that bitch."

"Can't see why. She's too skinny for my taste."

Slocum knew they were talking about Melody. He got to the far side of the tracks running onto the trestle, then lay down, letting the steel rail shield him partially. In the darkness they wouldn't notice that the one rail seemed a bit thicker than the other—he hoped.

Wall and two men walked past him, never seeing him. Slocum rose up enough to watch them vanish over the edge of the canyon rim. It took him several seconds to realize they had taken a path down the gorge wall rather than falling to the river below.

He cautiously trailed them, seeing Wall and the others fifty feet below on a small ledge.

"Get your ass on down there and don't you so much as lay one finger on her, you hear?" Wall ordered. "If you do, and I find out about it, I'll flay you alive. If Parsons finds out, well, he learned some nasty tricks from the Apaches when he was down New Mexico way. I doubt he'd be hesitant about showing you some of them."

"There's no need to threaten me, Emmett. You told me to let her be."

"Later," Wall promised, "when we get the government money, *then* you can have her." He laughed harshly. "Then we *all* can have her as often as we like."

"Until she wears out," the man with Wall joked. They laughed uproariously at this. Slocum settled down, trying to fade into the hillside. The man Wall had singled out to be Melody's guard vanished from sight, his boots grating against stone as he made his way down the trail. Wall and the other man came back up the steep, rocky slope. Again they passed within a few feet of Slocum and never knew he was there.

Slocum watched Wall's receding back and itched to put a slug in it. He kept telling himself the time would come soon. But now it was time to get Melody away from them. When Wall and his henchman had vanished and the general din in the camp went up in celebration at the Rocky Mountain Rail Line's victory, Slocum started down the trail.

He found the rocky ledge where the others had stopped to talk. It was hardly more than ten feet long and hardly three feet wide—and it was the biggest flat area in sight. The trail narrowed even more until it was hardly eighteen inches wide. Slocum crouched carefully and checked to be sure he wasn't on a wild-goose chase. He didn't think the other man could have found a different way down the canyon's sheer face, but Slocum wasn't sure in the dark.

Scuff marks and bright shiny scratches on the rock showed that more than one man had passed this way recently. Slocum couldn't imagine how they got Melody down such a narrow path. The feisty woman would have thrown herself off the cliff in the hopes of taking one of her captors with her.

Edging along the stone face, Slocum got past the narrow part and onto a wider trail. Here there was enough dirt to make the going less noisy. His boots didn't click and echo on the rock, which made the going safer. He occasionally looked over the verge, trying to find the man preceding him on the trail. Slocum heard the rush of the river below and the whistle of wind along the canyon walls, but he didn't find any trace of the other man, swallowed by shadow.

It took Slocum almost an hour to reach the bottom. The longer he was on the trail, the edgier he got. If the man who had spoken with Wall was a replacement guard, that meant Slocum might bump into the guard who had been relieved coming up from the bottom. He reached a gravelly stretch at the bottom of the canyon, though, without seeing anyone. He held his rifle at ready, wary of every slight sound that came over the rush of the river. Slocum ducked his head slightly as spray from the river threatened to blind him with its fine mist, not that it mattered in the almost impenetrable darkness at the bottom of the gorge. The moon would have to come up to light the way; too few stars showed through the heavy cloud layer above to give even a hint of illumination.

He almost ran into a base on the trestle. This startled Slocum. He hadn't thought the supporting timber would run all the way to the bottom of the gorge. Better to blast support into the rock face four hundred feet up.

Then he revised his guess. This wasn't the bridge he had run into, it was piece of a flatcar that had crashed into the canyon. He grinned as he remembered watching it tumble off the unfinished trestle, taking part of the structure with it. Slocum looked up and tried to see the bridge itself but couldn't. The pieces of flatcar were strewn around, partly in the raging river and partly on the graveled bank.

The constant noise and his diverted attention almost betrayed him. The guard who had been relieved came swinging along, not ten feet away. Only his drunken condition kept him from being more alert. Slocum ducked behind the piece of flatcar bed and waited until the man had passed, vanishing in seconds into the misty dark. Slocum considered taking him out, then decided against it. The long climb to the top of the cliff would wear him out, and he wouldn't be looking for any trouble. If Wall waited for the man to report in and he never showed up, the foreman would know there was trouble brewing.

Slocum pushed on, secure in knowing he was close to invisible in the ever-present mist and night. He was guided by the light shining through a partially opened door not fifty yards away. Slocum approached cautiously, knowing he'd have only one chance at rescuing Melody. There was no place to run if he failed.

"You're a pig," he heard Melody yell. "Stay away from me."

"Aw, Missy, I ain't so bad. You'll get to like me. Emmett says I can have you when your daddy's railroad is all rusted and forgotten."

Slocum moved more quickly. He wasn't sure if there was only the single guard. If so, his attack would be quick and easy. If he had to fight more than one man, he'd have to move fast and not miss with a single shot.

Slocum got to the door of the ramshackle cabin and peered in quickly, ducking back almost instantly. He had gotten enough of a look at the single room to know where everyone was. Melody had only the one guard with her, and there didn't seem to be evidence of any other. He saw only one battered tin coffee cup on the table and the small black cast iron pot dangling on its hook over the fire wasn't enough for two men. Slocum doubted if they were feeding Melody too much; keep her weak, break her spirit.

"If not now, then later," the guard said. "Emmett's promised me."

"To hell with Wall!" Melody raged. Slocum heard heavy rattling and scraping. He chanced a second look. Melody was tied to a chair and bounced it up and down trying to kick out at the man standing beside her. Her legs were fastened by rope loops and her hands were bound securely behind the chair. She wasn't going to do anything but get rope burns from such an attack.

"John!" she blurted.

Slocum acted as fast as he ever had. He spun into the room, rifle leveled. He fired just as the guard turned, his hand going for his six-shooter.

Slocum wasn't sure exactly what happened. The guard held a coal oil lamp in his left hand and, in going for his six-gun, the lamp got tangled up in his left sleeve. It crashed to the floor as fabric tore. Slocum used the confusion to fire. The bullet tore fairly and caught the man in the center of the chest. He staggered back, turned, and fell.

In a flash, fire swallowed the man, starting with his left sleeve and spreading to the rest of his clothing. The fire jumped from the man to the table—or so it seemed to Slocum.

"John, get me loose! I can't move."

Slocum went to Melody, checked the ropes, and saw that the quickest way of getting her free was to use his knife. He savagely slashed at the ropes. She screamed, then collapsed in his arms when he got her free.

"That hurt, John. My wrists are bleeding."

The rope had soaked up some of her blood from earlier attempts to get free. Cutting the rope away as he had was worse than pulling a plaster bandage off, but it had to be done. The flames licked at the cabin walls and threatened to trap them.

"Out," he ordered. "We don't have time to stand around." He shoved her toward the door, following closely. She tried to go back into the cabin, like a horse drawn to fire, but he shoved her hard enough to send her sprawling outside.

"My spare clothes. They brought some for me. They're inside."

"I'll buy you more when we get to a city," Slocum said. He scooped her up and half-carried, half-dragged her away from the cabin. Sparks rose from the inferno. Slocum glanced up and hoped that the fire would carry over to the trestle, though he doubted it. The spray from the raging river would keep all but the fiercest sparks from getting more than a few yards into the air.

"God, John, it's good to see you. I—I didn't think I would see you again, after what Papa said and did."

"He called out the law in Denver on me. I just missed being arrested."

"I know. I'm so sorry." She clung to him and made him believe her.

"We can't just stand here. We've got to leave right now."

"Can't we rest a few minutes? I'm so exhausted. They wouldn't let me sleep, and when I did nod off, it was so uncomfortable."

"We've got to go *now*," he insisted. "Wall can see the fire from the gorge rim and will send down men to investigate. We've got to be gone by then." He tried to see across the river to the far wall. There might be a path leading up there, too. Slocum decided it wouldn't do them much good since the river was almost impassable. For this late in the year it was still swollen with fast-running water.

"Just a minute, John. I'm so tired, so very tired." Melody sat with her head between her knees. Slocum paced back and forth, champing at the bit to get moving. It might take an hour for Wall's men to get to the bottom of the gorge—or they might get down quicker. Slocum wondered if they didn't have a windlass and rope that could lower men and supplies to work on the trestle. A few hundred feet more of rope and gunmen could be lowered in only a few minutes. For Melody Bergstrom, Wall might just risk such a maneuver.

"Now," Slocum said. "We're going downstream. We can't cross the river here, and I don't see any reason to go upstream."

"There might be a way up a few miles down the canyon," Melody said. "I didn't study the topographic maps too carefully, but I remember that the river bends back in an oxbow."

"That might give us some way of climbing," Slocum allowed.

Melody struggled to her feet and stumbled along beside Slocum. He kept her moving, even as he craned his neck to catch any sight of pursuit from five hundred feet above. It might have been his imagination, but Slocum thought he saw a dozen flickering lights along the cliff face, but every time he tried to stop and be sure, Melody tried to go to sleep. He thought it was better to keep moving and not be sure. It was one hell of a long night for both of them.

19

"I can't go on, John. I'm dead on my feet." Melody Bergstrom sank to the rocky canyon floor, her back pressed against a slime-slick boulder. Shaking her head, she said, "I can't go on. Really. I've been through too much."

"You'll have to go through more," Slocum said. "We've got to find a way up the canyon walls. And I don't know if Wall is on our trail. I haven't seen anyone behind us, but—" He let the sentence dangle. He was worried. Wall wouldn't take more than an hour to get to the bottom of the gorge with his men. When they found the cabin burned and only one body inside, they'd start hunting for Melody. He might suspect Slocum had come to the woman's aid, or not. It didn't matter. He'd want the only hold Parsons had over Clarence Bergstrom back. Without Melody, Parsons couldn't enforce his blackmail to stop construction on the Denver and Utah Railroad.

"What happened?" she asked. "Back at camp? I know it must be terrible. I heard shooting and explosions and it was all so jumbled."

"Gus is dead," Slocum said straight out. He saw no reason to whitewash it or beat around the bush. "I'm not

154

sure who did it, but Parsons definitely ordered the raid."

"Wall taunted me with Gus's death. I didn't really believe him. I thought he was just trying to scare me."

She clung to Slocum tightly. "It worked. I've never been more frightened in my life."

"We've got to find a trail to the rim and get back to the construction camp," he said.

"John, in a little while. Please."

He decided he had to tell her the whole truth. And he did. Melody sat back, her brown eyes wide with horror.

"Papa can't stop! We're almost through. Another week of work at the outside and we'd win!"

"You don't think the trestle will hold?"

"Impossible," she said firmly. "I caught sight of the way they blasted the supports on the gorge wall. Using that configuration, there's no steel beam strong enough to support the weight of a fully loaded engine. And Parsons didn't use a steel beam. He used green timbers. The whole bridge will come tumbling down if a real train tries crossing."

"Then it's all the more important you get back to camp safely and let your father know," Slocum said.

"Was he badly hurt?"

Slocum could only nod. He couldn't find the right words to tell the woman her father was going to be a cripple for the rest of his life. But he did say, "He's willing to give up the only thing he's got—the Denver and Utah—for you."

She buried her face in his shoulder and wept softly. Slocum held her close until she stopped crying. She turned her tear-stained face up and looked at him. "I'm so glad you're here, John."

They kissed. And Slocum knew they weren't going to be moving on for some time. It seemed crazy, and yet it was right. They had been through so much, but Melody was the one who had suffered the greatest losses. Gus Maguire had been a lifelong friend; Slocum had known the jovial Irishman only a short while. And Melody's father was badly hurt, both in body and soul. He was seeing everything he had worked so hard for slipping away, including his daughter's life.

She had to get the hurt out; she had to bury her fear so she could carry on. And Slocum helped her. His lips crushed into hers and returned some of the mounting passion. Melody gasped and broke away, leaning back.

"It's rocky here, John. What are we going to do?"

Slocum silently lifted her, his hands under her armpits, and sat her on the rock. Melody almost slipped off it, then found a more secure position. She leaned back on her elbows, her eyes aglow. Slocum reached out and touched her cheek, then let his hand run down her jawline to her neck, and then more slowly lower.

Melody gasped when his hand cupped her left breast. He felt the pounding of her heart through the cloth. He teased and toyed and stroked. For his effort he got a hard little nubbin beneath the folds of cloth. He caught the hardness between thumb and forefinger and pinched lightly. The lovely woman gasped with pleasure. He repeated this on the other breast.

"I need you," she sighed, supporting herself on her elbows. "Don't stop now. I need you, I need you so damned much!"

Slocum's wandering hands worked down the front of her torn, stained dress and found the skirt. He lifted as the woman spread her legs apart. Slocum hesitated when he found that she wasn't wearing anything under her skirt.

"It's not that way, John. They caught me while I was taking a bath. I didn't have time to dress fully. None of them harmed me, not like that."

Melody grabbed his arms and pulled him close for a long kiss. Slocum felt the world slipping away as he was totally caught up in the wonder of this woman. The mist drizzling down from the river only added to the stimulation he felt. Tiny rivulets of water ran from his hair and down his face, dripping off his chin onto exposed flesh. Melody giggled as he teased her with the continual dripping.

"More, John. Give me more."

"Are you sure?" he asked. The expression on the woman's face told him this wasn't as much a lovemaking as it was a way to forget for a few minutes. She would enjoy the physical sensations as they rippled through her body, but the mental release was what Melody Bergstrom sought at this instant.

He worked his way forward, positioning himself between her legs. He fumbled a few seconds getting his cross-draw holster off and letting it fall to the ground. Then he worked at the buttons on his fly. Melody was stroking his damp hair, pushing it back from his face, dipping her fingers into his ears, tracing the lobes and only then moving forward to touch his pursed lips.

She gasped when she felt the first touch of his hot shaft. He paused for a few seconds, gathering his strength. Then he moved into her softly yielding interior. He was surrounded by tightness and warmth. He revelled in the feel, the way her satin muscles tensed and relaxed on his hidden length, the tiny movements she made with her hips, rising and falling, twisting from side to side. He thought he was going to be broken off inside when she threw herself back suddenly, ramming her crotch down fully onto his.

"Move, damn you. Don't just stand there. Burn me up. I need it!"

He gripped her buttocks and lifted them off the rock. Squeezing and kneading those fleshy half-moons caused even more agitation in the woman. She thrashed around, but Slocum held on tight. He pulled almost out of her, paused, and then moved back in with a slow, deliberate stroke. Warmth mounted along his manhood and he felt his balls tensing. But he wanted to draw this out for Melody. She needed release and he wanted it to be complete.

She tried to reach up and grab his shoulders, but the way she sprawled back on the rock made this impossible. Her hips bucked and gyrated like a bronco being broken. Slocum kept moving with the same careful stroke, though he was hard-pressed to restrain himself. He felt his balls coming to a quick boil, as if it had been a dozen years since he'd had a woman.

Melody was gorgeous and she was well-versed in ways of pleasuring a man. Slocum doubted she was consciously squeezing and relaxing her strong inner muscles, but it worked on him constantly. He began speeding up. His hips levered back and forth with more power. He ground himself into her crotch, stimulating her even further, then pulled back quickly. Friction mounted, and he knew he was going to burn up inside her clutching tunnel of female flesh.

"Yes, John, yes, yes," she sobbed. She balled her fists so tightly drops of blood began dripping from her cut palms. Slocum picked up the pace even more, his control vanishing at the sight of her arousal. He stroked and lifted her buttocks, then snapped her entirely off the rock and supported her entire weight.

She sagged a little, then threw her arms around his neck and began kissing him wildly. Slocum had to rock back and forth to drive in and out of the woman, but the effort was worth it. He felt her quiver, then go tense. She let out a final shudder and clung to him limply. Continuing his bouncing motion robbed him of his control. He felt the rush begin, held it off for an instant, then gave in. He spewed forth into her clinging interior while she almost strangled him with her arms around his strong neck.

"More, John, give me more," she said sleepily.

He released Melody and put her down on the ground. She was asleep before he had a chance to button his trousers. Slocum stared at her, worried about pursuit, then shook his head. They couldn't go on, not with Melody so tired. This was good for her—for both of them if they wanted to make any time later.

"Sleep," he said, covering her up the best he could. Slocum hefted his rifle and backtracked to be sure Wall and his killers weren't on their trail.

• • •

The climb had been arduous without much of a trail to use, but Melody and Slocum had made good time reaching the top of the gorge. Cut and scratched from the sharp rock, they almost collapsed at the top. Slocum had to look back. It was well nigh sundown the day after he had rescued her from the cabin and the bottom of Grand Gorge was again swaddled in shadows. No trace of Wall or pursuit, Slocum decided. He kept a careful watch for another few minutes but saw no hint of torches moving along the bottom. He might have seen reflections, fireflies, or just plain hallucinations darting about, but he discounted them all as too insignificant to mean anything.

"We're a few miles from the base camp," Melody said. "We can catch the freight train up into Widowmaker Pass and get going on laying track again. Papa will want to get the crew working around the clock now that I'm back."

Slocum said nothing to douse the woman's newfound enthusiasm. She knew her father was hurt bad but she hadn't seen him. During the war Slocum had seen men with less injury turn inward and become little more than human vegetables, staring at nothing all day long. Occasional movement was all that told anyone they still lived. He hoped Bergstrom had fought away the depression of losing friends, daughter, and railroad, but Slocum didn't think so. When he had spoken with the railroad baron, he had been a broken man.

"Anything below?" she asked.

"Don't see anything. We've got a few hours of hiking ahead, but I'm a bit wobbly on my feet. It's been a spell since I ate."

"I cannot remember when I last ate, either," Melody said. "Are you thinking of hunting? It might be better to just push on."

Slocum considered the merits of getting some grub now or exerting the effort and reaching a camp with a cook and a full larder. It might not be great food, but it would be better than any scrawny rabbit or ground squirrel he might bag.

"Let's hike," he said, helping her to her feet.

They reached Bergstrom's camp two hours later, just as the sun dipped behind the tallest peaks to the west. A single ray of light shone through Widowmaker Pass, as if lighting the way. Slocum wondered if it showed where the Denver and Utah Railroad was bound or was only giving silent tribute to the men who had already died trying to push through the treacherous pass.

"Miss Melody!" went up the cry the instant a worker saw her. "You're back. You and Slocum are back!"

In seconds they were surrounded by cheering men. Slocum had to protect Melody from the crush of unwashed, powerful bodies all trying to get close enough to clap her on the back or shake her hand.

"Papa," she shouted. "Where's Papa?"

The loud cheering died down and the crowd parted as if by magic. One man pointed toward the luxurious coach on the siding. No one spoke as Melody hurried to see her father.

A heavy hand grabbed Slocum's shoulder and held him back. "Does she know?" Slocum could only nod. His mouth was parched and he was shaking from lack of food.

He managed to croak out, "Get us some grub, will you? And something fit to drink. We're going to be talking with Mr. Bergstrom for quite a while."

"I don't think so," the burly Irishman said. "He's not been up to much since—you know."

"I know. Get the food." Slocum trailed Melody into the rail car, giving her a few minutes to get the crying out of the way. She clutched her father's destroyed body and clung to him as if he could save her from falling into a huge abyss. Slocum wanted to tell her their roles had been reversed. She had to save him now.

"Slocum, you saved her. Thank you. I'm sorry for what I thought." Tears ran down Bergstrom's cheeks.

"That's behind us now, sir," Slocum said. "Since Melody's no longer a prisoner, you can go ahead with laying the track through the pass."

"No. No, I won't. This is taking too much out of me. Parsons would only do something even worse."

"What, Papa, what worse could he do? He killed Gus. He crippled you!"

"He'll try to hurt you again, dearest. I can't allow that."

"Seems to me he'll try, no matter what," Slocum said. "With Melody gone, Parsons will be all fired up to kill anything that moves. I say we get ready for him, and we keep laying track. You've got him beat."

"No, no," said Bergstrom. "You went on about that before, back at his camp. It's not so. His trestle—"

"Will collapse, Papa!" exclaimed Melody. "It won't hold a fully loaded train, even one of his toy narrow-gage models."

"She's right. You're about a week away from getting over the pass. The first time Parsons runs a real trainload over his bridge, the game's up."

"The risk," muttered Bergstrom. "Too great. Can't risk you like this again, Melody. I'll order the engine in from Denver and we can go back to—"

"We can go back to hell!" she shrieked. She shot to her feet and stared angrily at her father. "We've been through too much to give up. Gus Maguire died for the Denver and Utah. If you won't ramrod this road through, then by God, I will!"

Slocum had seen such fire before, and there was no stopping the person filled with it. It made Melody all the more beautiful in his eyes, in spite of the grime and torn clothing and numerous tiny bruises and cuts on her arms and face.

"I agree. If you won't, we will. I don't know anything about being a foreman, but I know something about being a powder monkey. We can blast the rest of the way."

"And I'll be the foreman." Melody Bergstrom crossed her arms as if daring her father to protest.

Instead, Slocum asked, "Will the men stand for it? They're fired up that we're back, but will they take orders from a woman?"

"Let's find out." Melody swung around and went to the back platform of the car. Dozens of men were still gathered there. She paused for a moment to let the buzz die down, then cleared her throat.

The men seemed to tense, waiting for the news. And Melody gave it to them with both barrels.

"My father won't push the Denver and Utah through Widowmaker Pass." A deep sigh went up and grumbles of protest started. She cut them off. "But, by damn, *I* will see this railroad to the other side of the divide. Are you with me?"

The roar was deafening. Slocum stood back, just inside the door to the car. She was a real firebrand and had the men whipped into doing her bidding. Slocum turned and looked at Clarence Bergstrom. The man hunched over, a beaten man just waiting to die.

Bergstrom was defeated, but Melody was not—and the loud hoorays from her crew made Slocum think she just might finish the railroad ahead of Anthony Parsons.

20

"Before sundown, Parsons is going to hear about work starting again," Slocum said, riding along in the rear of the rattling freight car. Melody perched next to him, decked out in men's canvas trousers and a denim work shirt that molded itself perfectly to her body. She tossed her hair and let the wind carry it back from her face. Slocum wasn't sure he had ever seen anyone lovelier.

"I don't care. We can beat him, John. You said so."

"I'm no expert when it comes to building a railroad." He looked into her brown eyes and asked, "Are you?"

"I will be." She turned away from him and closed her eyes against the rush of the cold air blowing past them. Slocum knew that it would rest entirely on her shoulders. Clarence Bergstrom was in no condition to continue the fight; Parsons had broken him in both body and spirit.

"How much more blasting needs to be done?" Slocum asked. "I can help there, if you need it, but someone's been doing a fair job from the look of it." The engine huffed and puffed and got up the steep slope leading into Widowmaker Pass. Slocum saw the bright gouges of rock ripped from the mountainside. The blasting might not have been expert, but it was effective enough to completely open the way that the other railroad company had started.

"I think only a few more blasts are needed. We're actually close to being through. The rail bed needs work, but it always does. We can lay the track and worry about the underpinning after we have the government money in our bank account."

She turned and looked at him. Melody had gotten to know him well enough. She said, "You don't want to waste time blowing up the side of the mountain, do you? What are you thinking, John?"

"We can beat Parsons fair and square. I don't doubt that."

"But you don't think he's going to play fairly, do you?"

"He hasn't up till now," Slocum said. "I don't want to harp on it, but he's ruined your father. He's not about doing that to you."

"He can't break my spirit. There's nothing he can do." She set her jaw and for an instant Slocum almost believed her. But he knew better. How would she enjoy being sold as a whore in some dockside dive where anyone with a nickel could have her? Melody had no idea what a man like Anthony Parsons was capable of doing to her, if he got the idea into his head that he wanted her to crawl.

"We've got to carry the fight back to him. He might get lucky and keep that bridge up long enough to get over Grand Gorge."

"Maybe," she said doubtfully. "The government inspector's due out from Denver in a few days. He'll be waiting in Cameron."

"Now's the time to do whatever it takes to win the contract," Slocum pressed. "Are you that ruthless?"

"Are you?" Melody spoke lightly, but when she saw the coldness in his eyes, she shivered and turned away. This solidified Slocum's opinion of her. She talked big, but if Parsons really started working on her, she'd cave in quickly. In a low voice, she added. "Maybe you are, John."

"Count on it," Slocum said. "I'm as hard as I have to be—and I still want Emmett Wall."

"The law can take care of him."

"The law doesn't exist out here. We're the law. *This* is." He touched the ebony handle of his Colt Navy.

"I wish it didn't have to be this way."

"You know it does. Think of your father. Think of Gus."

"What do you have in mind?"

Slocum wasn't sure he wanted to tell her. He had waltzed through the Rocky Mountain Rail Line camp too many times for them not to be waiting for him again. He had to try something different, and what he wanted to do was better not mentioned to Melody if anything went wrong. Parsons would never let her slip entirely free, but she could always claim that Slocum had gone crazy and acted on his own.

Slocum smiled crookedly. It had been a month of Sundays since he'd held up a train.

"All right, John. Go on and do whatever you want. But—" She reached out to him, her hand trembling.

"Don't get killed," he finished for her. "That's not the way I do things." He bent over and gave her a quick kiss and was getting ready for a second one, when the train lurched to a halt. They had reached the farthest track laid through Widowmaker Pass.

Slocum touched her cheek, then jumped from the train to supervise the unloading. He spoke with several men who had been learning the blasting by doing it and gave them some advice on how to get better results with less explosive, then got back on the train just as it was preparing for the return trip to the base camp.

"John, I wish you weren't going. We can really use you here." Melody Bergstrom looked up at him with tears in her eyes. She had courage, but he saw fear in her eyes. She wasn't sure she could be the foreman for such a bunch of roughnecks.

"You'll do fine. It's less than a week to the other side. Remember that. You're almost there."

The train whistled, lurched, and began moving back down the pass. Slocum hung out the side and waved, then ducked back when a sheer rock face threatened to knock him off. As the train raced back down the slope, he plotted and planned. It was difficult for one man to hold up a train, but what he intended to do wasn't exactly a holdup. Not exactly.

Slocum studied what he had done to the narrow-gage track leading into Parsons's camp. Ties had been piled across the steel rails and soaked with kerosene. Up and down the track were large rocks and odd bits of rusted equipment Emmett Wall had seen fit to leave rather than take on into his camp. Slocum tried to guess how much the debris weighed and gave up. It didn't matter that much. He paced back and forth, trying to guess how far it was to the Rocky Mountain Rail Line camp. More than ten miles, he reckoned. Just enough for what he wanted to do.

He placed a foot on one rail and felt vibration. It was time for him to put his plan into action. He got a lucifer from his pocket, worked it from its tin box, and ignited it. When a three-inch-high flame showed, Slocum tossed it onto the ties. They flared and blazed merrily. The fire gave him a moment's warmth, then he moved away. He wanted to be up high so he could fire down on the train.

Getting to his post just in time, Slocum saw the narrow-gage engine rounding the bend. The engineer shouted and applied the brakes immediately. Long blue sparks from the straining steel wheels crawled into the dusk like insane cockroaches as the train came to a halt less than five feet from the burning ties.

"What the hell's going on?" shouted the engineer. "You, get out there and pry those ties off the road."

Slocum's first shot took the engineer in the shoulder, spinning him around and making him fall out of the cab. The fireman stood and stared. By this time others from the train rushed forward to see what was happening.

"We've got you surrounded, and we don't mind killing—unless you do what you're told."

"What's that?" stammered the fireman, a youth hardly in his teens.

The conductor came up and tried to restore some order among the milling workers. Slocum laid him low with a shot to the leg.

"What's in the freight cars?" he called down.

"Not much. Just some supplies. The cars are mostly empty," the fireman replied.

"Get them loading the cars," Slocum ordered.

"How's that? Load what? Mister, there ain't nothing out here but rock and all that rusty machinery."

"Start with that," Slocum said. "Then we'll think a mite more on it."

A few well-placed rounds kept the men working, puzzled at the odd robbery. Slocum made his way along a ridge and checked the workmen's progress. When they had filled all of one freight car and most of another, he decided he was pushing his luck. Sooner or later one of the men would get to feeling put upon and Slocum would have to kill him.

"All right, everybody but the fireman out to the side of the track." Slocum did a quick count and made sure everyone was there. "Now, start walking. Denver's not far if you keep at it. And take the engineer and conductor with you." He fired until his rifle was empty to get the men moving.

Depending on his trusty Colt, Slocum jumped onto the top of a freight car and worked his way forward to the engine. The fireman stood shaking, sure that he was going to die.

"Mister, I ain't done nothing to you. I—"

"Shut up and stoke the boiler. How much wood can it take?"

"Don't rightly know since I never tried it. We need a constant steam head, not—"

"Don't go telling me what you usually do. You're going to fire the engine up to the most pressure its boiler can hold. Do you understand?"

"But the track is blocked."

Slocum peered out of the cab and saw that the ties had burned away to a few embers. The train could push them off the track with no effort.

"Feed the fire. We're going to highball into camp."

"Highball? Mister, there's not enough room to stop."

"Then you'd better think about jumping—after you stoke this boiler." Slocum pointed his six-shooter in the boy's general direction. A lump the size of a goose egg bobbed in the youth's throat, then he began shoveling wood into the firebox as if his life depended on it. Slocum looked over the controls. They were simple enough for all the prestige attached to being a railroad engineer. He tapped the pressure gauge with the butt of his pistol, then settled onto the hard wood seat and looked out into the darkness.

"Mister, the needle's getting to the red line. Mr. Hotchkiss always told me to let him know when that happened."

"Thank you," Slocum said. He released the brake, and the train began moving slowly. He pushed the control lever all the way forward, and the train almost leapt off the track as power flooded onto the drive wheels. "And keep throwing wood into the box."

"Yes, sir," the fireman said, still eyeing the gun in Slocum's hand.

Slocum had figured he was ten miles outside Parsons's camp. It took more than twenty minutes with the heavier load trailing behind the engine to reach the construction site. The train came out of a notch, hit a level stretch, and started to pick up speed.

"Keep stoking," Slocum ordered.

"Mister, the switch. It might be thrown for a siding. We might be derailed." The fireman looked nervously at the pressure gauge. The needle hovered just at the red line showing the point where the boiler could take no more.

"Do as you're told." Slocum worried that the boy might be right. Did Emmett Wall keep the main line closed, just to be sure nothing crossed the trestle? The engine pounded harder and harder and hit the downslope going toward the fragile trestle. The wind whistled past Slocum's face. He turned to the frightened fireman and motioned with his pistol. "Go on, jump."

The boy didn't have to be told twice. He dived headlong off the engine. Slocum wasn't sure how fast the train was moving, but it had to be better than forty miles an hour. With the load being pulled behind it, the trestle ought to collapse just right.

Slocum worried again about the switch as he saw a green and red light on the switch handle. He didn't know what it meant. The siding came closer and closer and Slocum prepared to get off the train if the engine was diverted.

The narrow-gage train rushed past the siding and toward the trestle. Slocum saw the horror on the workers' faces as he rumbled past. He took scant pleasure in it. He had to judge how to do this just right without getting off too soon or waiting too long and plunging into Grand Gorge with the engine.

He yanked the control lever to its wide-open position and then heaved himself off the train. He hit hard and rolled, coming to his feet. He half-turned and lost his balance, stumbling from the momentum of his fall. He landed flat on his belly, turned so he could see the train steaming across the bridge.

At first Slocum thought nothing was going to happen. The train got to the center of the trestle and kept on going. Then he heard a sound like a thousand banshees crying for someone's soul. The shriek increased in pitch until it deafened him. The train looked as if it was on ice, sliding to one side as the trestle collapsed under its weight. First one car slipped from the tracks, then another and another until only the engine remained.

Slocum watched in fascination as the steam engine appeared to drop backward into the gorge, taking a large part of the trestle with it. Slowly, slowly, slowly the engine retraced its path and then vanished from sight. Less than five seconds later there was a huge explosion as the engine's boiler split and blew up at the bottom of the canyon.

He got his feet under him and stared at the bridge. He couldn't believe his scheme had been so successful. Only twigs remained to show that Parsons had ever started a bridge across Grand Gorge.

Slocum shook the dirt off and turned when a cold voice said, "This is gonna give me more pleasure than you can imagine, Slocum."

Emmett Wall's six-shooter cocked.

21

Slocum knew he didn't stand a chance of drawing and firing in time. Wall had the drop on him. Slocum's legs acted like springs, shoving him downhill, so that he rolled toward the canyon rim. A slug ripped off his hat and sent it flying. A second one pinked his leg. A third went wild and whistled off into the night. By this time Slocum was fighting to keep from following the engine into the deep gorge. He finally got some purchase with the toes of his boots. A fourth slug kicked dirt up in front of his face, momentarily blinding him. He fell flat and dragged his Colt Navy up.

"I'll get you, just like I back-shot that no-good Gus Maguire. And I done Bergstrom good, too. You're buzzard meat, Slocum, you're dead. You've ruined me and—"

Wall moved just enough to outline himself against a large bonfire blazing in the center of the camp. His long mustache was perfectly silhouetted, and it jerked up and down as the man's jaw moved. Never would the foreman make a better target. Slocum's pistol centered and he fired. Wall jerked. A fifth shot dug itself into the ground. Slocum made sure that Wall would never get a sixth try at killing him. Three more slugs from Slocum's Colt sped into the night, each finding a target in the foreman's body.

Slocum got up and walked over to the fallen man. He stared at him for a moment. "You did it all, you sorry bastard. Now you've paid." He thought a moment, then fired again into the fallen man, just for the hell of it.

Slocum felt no victory. He had gotten his revenge on Wall, but there was a curiously hollow feel to it. The foreman was dead. He'd never kill again. That was the only retribution Slocum could see. If anything, Wall had died too fast and didn't have time to regret his murderous ways.

He wanted to plug Anthony Parsons through the gut, too, but a thought came to him that gave him more pleasure than killing the man ever could. Parsons's foreman was dead, and so was his railroad. Destroying the trestle gave the race to Clarence Bergstrom. Knowing that a foe he had thought was defeated had bested him would be far worse punishment than anything else Slocum could do to Parsons.

A loud shout went up from the camp. Slocum knew it was time to move on. He had done all the damage he could now. Becoming one with the shadows, he worked his way through the disorganized lines of guards Wall had thrown up to protect the construction site.

"There ought to have been more done to him," Melody Bergstrom declared. "He ought to *suffer* for all he's done."

"You can always sic the law on him. A man like that lives crooked and can't think of any other way to get through life. There's got to be other things he's done that'll turn up if you kick over enough rocks. And without the protection of money generated by a railroad, he might not be able to hide from the law." Slocum hoped Parsons was stewing in his own juices. They had pushed the Denver and Utah track through Widowmaker Pass in only five days. The eight miles on into Cameron seemed to take no time at all. The town had even gone so far as to build a station house for the road.

But only Slocum noticed that the lettering had been hastily painted over. It had originally read Rocky Mountain Rail Line and now carried the Denver and Utah name. The good people of Cameron hadn't put much store in Clarence Bergstrom or his determination to cross the divide with a full-sized track.

Slocum turned and looked at Melody. She beamed as she leaned out of the engine cab and waved to the people. They were moving slowly, testing the track as they went. Having the engine derailed here would be disastrous, but nothing like that happened. The train pulled into the station amid cheers and loud whistles. Half a dozen men dressed in suits and carrying huge piles of papers waited beside what was obviously the mayor of Cameron.

"Those must be the government agents," Slocum said. The small group had the look of every other official Slocum had ever seen. Not a one could think of anything original without looking it up first in his sheaf of papers.

"Yes, John, yes, they are, they are! I recognize the tall man as one who spoke with Papa back in Denver." The mayor of the town helped Melody to the platform and the real celebration began. Eager men and women crowded forward and kept Slocum away from the center of the festivities and from Melody's side.

Slocum hung back. This wasn't to his liking. Too many people pushing in real close, and a terrible roar from a bad brass band the town had scraped up from somewhere. In spite of the circus atmosphere, Slocum found himself staring at Melody Bergstrom. She was about the prettiest thing he had ever seen, and he knew what she'd say if he stayed. She'd want him to take Gus Maguire's job. The Denver and Utah had crossed the Rockies. Now there was the entire state of Utah to cover with steel rails.

Working on a railroad wasn't his kind of life. But there were other things to consider, if he stayed. He tried to think what it would be like being with Melody, but wanderlust kept getting in the way of his imagining. She was in hog heaven right now, basking in the praise of the townspeople and accepting the largess of the government for the hard work of getting a railroad over the country's rocky spine. She belonged. He didn't. When she signaled for the men to bring out her injured father, another cry went up from the crowd. Melody hugged the man and began her speechifying, telling how brave he was and how those who had died getting over Widowmaker Pass were heroes.

Melody Bergstrom held everyone spellbound with her beauty and rhetoric.

Slocum touched his shirt pocket. He had been paid the money owed him for the time he'd spent with the Denver and Utah. The gold was gone, but the greenbacks were almost as good. They rode better in his pocket. That was enough—more than enough since it fulfilled Gus Maguire's agreement with him. He dropped down on the far side of the train, went to the last freight car, and opened the door. A half dozen horses pawed at the wood floor, begging to be let loose. Slocum found his roan and jumped it to the ground. In five minutes he was saddled. In ten he was a mile south of Cameron. And in an hour he was wondering if he hadn't made a mistake.

But the sunlight was warm on his face and he didn't look back.

NELSON NYE

The Baron of Blood & Thunder

Two-time winner of the Western Writers of America's Golden Spur Award, and winner of the Levi Strauss Golden Saddleman Award . . . with over 50,000,000 copies of his books in print.

NELSON NYE

Author of RIDER ON THE ROAN, TROUBLE AT QUINN'S CROSSING, THE SEVEN SIX-GUNNERS, THE PARSON OF GUNBARREL BASIN, LONG RUN, GRINGO, THE LOST PADRE, TREASURE TRAIL FROM TUCSON, and dozens of others, is back with his most exciting Western adventure yet. . . .

THE LAST CHANCE KID

Born to English nobility, Alfred Addlington wants nothing more than to become an American cowboy. With his family's reluctant permission, Alfred becomes just that . . . and gets much more than he bargained for when he gets mixed up with horse thieves, crooked ranchers, and a band of prairie rats who implicate him in one crime after another!

Turn the page
for an exciting preview of
THE LAST CHANCE KID
by Nelson Nye!

My name is Alfred Addlington. Some may find it hard to believe I was born in New York City. I never knew my mother. Father is a lord; I suppose you would call him a belted earl. The family never cared for Mother. Marrying a commoner if you are of the nobility is far worse, it was felt, than murdering someone.

I was, of course, educated in England. As a child I'd been an avid reader, and always at the back of my mind was this horrible obsession to one day become a Wild West cowboy. I'd no need to run away— transportation was happily furnished. While I was in my seventeenth year my youthful peccadillos were such that I was put on a boat bound for America, made an allowance and told never to come back.

They've been hammering outside. I have been in this place now more than four months and would never have believed it could happen to me, but the bars on my window are truely there, and beyond the window they are building a gallows. So I'd better make haste if I'm to get this all down.

I do not lay my being here to a "broken home" or evil companions. I like to feel in some part it is only a matter of justice miscarried, though I suppose most any rogue faced with the rope is bound to consider himself badly used. But you shall judge for yourself.

Seventeen I was when put aboard that boat, and I had a wealth of experience before at nineteen this bad thing caught up with me.

So here I was again in America. In a number of ways it was a peculiar homecoming. First thing I did after clearing customs was get aboard a train that would take me into those great open spaces I'd so long been entranced with. It brought me to New Mexico and a town called Albuquerque, really an overgrown village from which I could see the Watermellon Mountains.

I found the land and the sky and the brilliant sunshine remarkably stimulating. Unlike in the British Midlands the air was clean and crisply invigorating. But no one would have me. At the third ranch I tried they said, "Too young. We got no time to break in a raw kid with roundup scarce two weeks away."

At that time I'd no idea of the many intricacies or the harsh realities of the cow business. You might say I had on a pair of rose-colored glasses. I gathered there might be quite a ruckus building up in Lincoln County, a sort of large-scale feud from all I could learn, so I bought myself a horse, a pistol and a J. B. Stetson hat and headed for the action.

In the interests of saving time and space I'll only touch on the highlights of these preliminaries, recording full details where events became of impelling importance.

Passing through Seven Oaks, I met Billy, a chap whose name was on everyone's tongue, though I could not think him worth half the talk. To me he seemed hard, mean spirited and stupid besides. He made fun of my horse, calling it a crowbait, declared no real gent would be found dead even near it. Turned out he knew of a first class mount he'd be glad to secure for me if I'd put one hundred dollars into his grubby hand. He was a swaggering sort I was glad to be rid of. Feeling that when in Rome one did as the

Romans, I gave him the hundred dollars, not expecting ever to see him again, but hoping in these strange surroundings I would not be taken for a gullible "greenhorn".

A few days later another chap, who said his name was Jesse Evans, advised me to steer clear of Billy. "A bad lot," he told me. "A conniving double-crosser." When I mentioned giving Billy the hundred dollars on the understanding he would provide a top horse, he said with a snort and kind of pitying look, "You better bid that money good-bye right now."

But three days later, true to his word, Billy rode up to the place I was lodging with a fine horse in tow. During my schooling back in England I had learned quite a bit about horses, mostly hunters and hacks and jumpers and a few that ran in "flat" races for purses, and this mount Billy fetched looked as good as the best. "Here, get on him," Billy urged. "See what you think, and if he won't do I'll find you another.

"He'll do just fine," I said, taking the lead shank, "and here's ten dollars for your kindness."

With that lopsided grin he took the ten and rode off.

I rode the new horse over to the livery and dressed him im my saddle and bridle while the proprietor eyed me with open mouth. "Don't tell me that's yours," he finally managed, still looking as if he couldn't believe what he saw.

"He surely is. Yes, indeed. Gave a hundred dollars for him."

Just as I was about to mount up, a mustached man came bustling into the place. "Stop right there!" this one said across the glint of a pistol. "I want to know what you're doing with the Major's horse. Speak up or it'll be the worse for you."

"What Major."

"Major Murphy. A big man around here."

"Never heard of him. I bought this horse for one hundred dollars."

"Bought it, eh? Got a bill of sale?"

"Well, no," I said. "Didn't think to ask for one."

I'd discovered by this time the man with the gun had a star on his vest. His expression was on the skeptical side. He wheeled on the liveryman. "You sell him that horse?"

"Not me! Came walkin' in here with it not ten minutes ago."

"I'm goin' to have to hold you, young feller," the man with the star said, pistol still aimed at my belt buckle. "A horse thief's the lowest scoundrel I know of."

A shadow darkened the doorway just then and Jesse Evans stepped in. "Hang on a bit, Marshall. I'll vouch for this button. If he told you he paid for this horse it's the truth. Paid it to Billy—I'll take my oath on it."

A rather curious change reshaped the marshall's features. "You sure of that, Evans?"

"Wouldn't say so if I wasn't."

The marshall looked considerably put out. "All right,'" he said to me, "looks like you're cleared. But I'm confiscatin' this yere horse; I'll see it gits back to the rightful owner. You're free to go, but don't let me find you round here come sundown." And he went off with the horse.

"Never mind," Evans said. "Just charge it up to experience. But was I you I'd take the marshal's advice and hunt me another habitation." And he grinned at me sadly "I mean pronto—right now."

Still rummaging my face, he said, scrubbing a fist across his own, "Tell you what I'll do," and led me away out of the livery-keeper's hearing. "I've got a reasonably good horse I'll let you have for fifty bucks. Even throw in a saddle— not so handsome as the one you had but durable and sturdy. You interested?"

Once stung, twice shy. "Let's see him," I said, and followed him out to a corral at the far edge of town. I looked the horse over for hidden defects but could find nothing wrong with it; certainly the animal should be worth fifty dollars. Firmly I said, "I'll be wanting a bill of sale."

"Of course," he chuckled. "Naturally." Fetching a little blue notebook out of a pocket, he asked politely, "What name do you go by?"

"My own," I said. "Alfred Addlington,"

He wrote it down with a flourish. "All right, Alfie." He tore the page from his book and I put it in my wallet while Jesse saddled and bridled my new posession. I handed him the money, accepted the reins and stepped into the saddle.

He said, "I'll give you a piece of advice you can take or cock a snook at. Notice you're packin' a pistol. Never put a hand anyplace near it without you're aimin' to use it. Better still," he said, looking me over more sharply, "get yourself a shotgun, one with two barrels. Nobody'll laugh at that kind of authority."

"Well, thanks. Where do I purchase one?"

"Be a-plenty at Lincoln if that's where you're headed. Any gun shop'll have 'em.

I thanked him again and, having gotten precise directions, struck out for the county seat feeling I'd been lucky to run across such a good Samaritain. I was a pretty fair shot with handgun or rifle but had discovered after much practice I could be killed and buried before getting my pistol into speaking position. So Evans's advice about acquiring a shotgun seemed additional evidence of the good will he bore me.

It was shortly after noon the next day when I came up the dirt road into Lincoln. For all practical purposes it was a one-street town, perhaps half a mile long, flanked by business establishments, chief amongst them being the two-storey Murphy-Dolan store building. I recall wondering if this was the Major whose stolen horse Billy'd sold me, later discovering it was indeed. Leaving my horse at a hitch rack I went inside to make inquiries about finding a job.

The gentleman I talked with had an Irish face underneath a gray derby. After listening politely he informed me he was Jimmie Dolan— the Dolan of the establishment, and could offer me work as a sort of handyman if such wasn't beneath my dignity. If I showed aptitude, he said, there'd be a better job later and he would start me off at fifty cents a day.

I told him I'd take it.

"If you've a horse there's a carriage shed back of the store where you can leave him and we'll sell you oats at a discount," he added.

"I'd been hoping to get on with some ranch," I said.

"A fool's job." said Dolan with a grimace. "Long hours, hard work, poor pay and no future," he assured me. "You string your bets with us and you'll get to be somebody while them yahoos on ranches are still punchin' cows."

I went out to feed, water and put up my new horse. There was a man outside giving it some pretty hard looks. "This your nag?" he asked as I came up.

"It most certainly is."

"Where'd you get it?"

"Bought it in Seven Oaks a couple days ago. Why?"

He eyed me some more. "Let's see your bill of sale, bub," and brushed back his coat to display a sheriff's badge pinned to his shirt.

I dug out the paper I had got for Evans. The sheriff studied it and then, much more searching, studied me. "Expect you must be new around here if you'd take Evans's word for anything. I'm taking it for granted you bought the horse in good faith, but I'm going to have to relieve you of it. This animal's the property of a man named Tunstall, stolen from him along with several others about a week ago."

I was pretty riled up. "This," I said angrily, "is the second stolen mount I've been relieved of in the past ten days. Don't you have any honest men in your bailiwick?"

"A few, son. Not many I'll grant you. You're talkin' to one now as it happens."

"Then where can I come by a horse that's not stolen?"

That blue stare rummage my face again. "You a limey?"

"If you mean do I hail from England, yes. I came here

hoping to get to be a cowboy but nobody'll have me."

He nodded. "It's a hard life, son, an' considerably underpaid. Takes time to learn, but you seem young enough to have plenty of that. How much did you give for the two stolen horses?"

"One hundred and fifty dollars."

He considered me again. "You're pretty green, I guess. Most horses in these parts sell for forty dollars."

"A regular Johnny Raw," I said bitterly.

"Well . . . a mite gullible," the sheriff admitted. "Reckon time will cure that if you live long enough. Being caught with a stolen horse hereabouts is a hangin' offense. Come along," he said. "I'll get you a horse there's no question about, along with a bona fide set of papers to prove it. Do you have forty dollars?"

I told him I had and, counting out the required sum, handed it to him. He picked up the reins of Tunstall's horse, and we walked down the road to a public livery and feed corral. The sheriff told the man there what we wanted and the fellow fetched out a good-looking sorrel mare.

"This here's a mite better'n average, Sheriff—oughta fetch eight. Trouble is these fool cowhands won't ride anythin' but geldin's. I guarantee this mare's a real goer. Try her out, boy. If you ain't satisfied, she's yours fer forty bucks."

The sheriff, meanwhile, had got my gear off Tunstall's horse. "Get me a lead shank," he said to the stableman. Transferring my saddle and bridle to the mare I swung onto her, did a few figure eights, put her into a lope, walked her around and proclaimed myself satisfied. The animal's name it seemed was Singlefoot. "She'll go all day at that rockin' chair gate," the man said. "Comfortable as two six-shooters in the same belt."

Thanking them both, I rode her over to the nearest café, tied her securely to the hitch pole in front of it and went in to put some food under my belt, pleased to see she looked very well alongside the tail-switchers already tied there.

If you enjoyed this book, subscribe now and get...

TWO FREE

A $7.00 VALUE—

If you would like to read more of the very best, most exciting, adventurous, action-packed Westerns being published today, you'll want to subscribe to True Value's Western Home Subscription Service.

Each month the editors of True Value will select the 6 very best Westerns from America's leading publishers for special readers like you. You'll be able to preview these new titles as soon as they are published, *FREE* for ten days with no obligation!

TWO FREE BOOKS

When you subscribe, we'll send you your first month's shipment of the newest and best 6 Westerns for you to preview. With your first shipment, two of these books will be yours as our introductory gift to you absolutely *FREE* (a $7.00 value), regardless of what you decide to do. If

you like them, as much as we think you will, keep all six books but pay for just 4 at the low subscriber rate of just $2.75 each. If you decide to return them, keep 2 of the titles as our gift. No obligation.

Special Subscriber Savings

When you become a True Value subscriber you'll save money several ways. First, all regular monthly selections will be billed at the low subscriber price of just $2.75 each. That's at least a savings of $4.50 each month below the publishers price. Second, there is never any shipping, handling or other hidden charges—*Free home delivery*. What's more there is no minimum number of books you must buy, you may return any selection for full credit and you can cancel your subscription at any time. A TRUE VALUE!

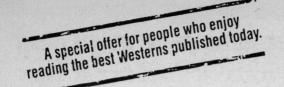